Bello:

hidden talent rediscovered!

Bello is a digital only imprint of Pan Macmillan,
established to breathe new life into previously published,
classic books.

At Bello we believe in the timeless power of the imagination,
of good story, narrative and entertainment and we want to use
digital technology to ensure that many more readers
can enjoy these books into the future.

We publish in ebook and Print on Demand formats
to bring these wonderful books to new audiences.

About Bello:

www.panmacmillan.com/imprints/bello

About the author:

www.panmacmillan.com/author/andrewgarve

Andrew Garve

Andrew Garve is the pen name of Paul Winterton (1908–2001). He was born in Leicester and educated at the Hulme Grammar School, Manchester and Purley County School, Surrey, after which he took a degree in Economics at London University. He was on the staff of *The Economist* for four years, and then worked for fourteen years for the *London News Chronicle* as reporter, leader writer and foreign correspondent. He was assigned to Moscow from 1942–5, where he was also the correspondent of the BBC's Overseas Service.

After the war he turned to full-time writing of detective and adventure novels and produced more than forty-five books. His work was serialized, televised, broadcast, filmed and translated into some twenty languages. He is noted for his varied and unusual backgrounds – which have included Russia, newspaper offices, the West Indies, ocean sailing, the Australian outback, politics, mountaineering and forestry – and for never repeating a plot.

Andrew Garve was a founder member and first joint secretary of the Crime Writers' Association.

Andrew Garve

THE SEA MONKS

BELL

First published in 1963 by William Collins Sons & Co Ltd

This edition published 2012 by Bello
an imprint of Pan Macmillan, a division of Macmillan Publishers Limited
Pan Macmillan, 20 New Wharf Road, London N1 9RR
Basingstoke and Oxford
Associated companies throughout the world

www.panmacmillan.com/imprints/bello
www.curtisbrown.co.uk

ISBN 978-1-4472-1534-9 EPUB
ISBN 978-1-4472-1533-2 POD

Visit **www.panmacmillan.com** to read more about all our books
and to buy them. You will also find features, author interviews and
news of any author events, and you can sign up for e-newsletters
so that you're always first to hear about our new releases.

Chapter One

The two loitering young men had already marked down the car they were going to take. It was one of a dozen or more parked at the kerb by people paying Sunday evening visits to Salmouth's quietest suburb. It was a Vaxhall, a popular family model, grey like the February fog that shrouded it, new enough to be reliable—and the trusting owner had left it unlocked with the ignition key still in the dash-board. Just asking for it. . . .

Under a street lamp, the young men stopped to check the time.

One was square and strongly built, with a muscular neck and powerful shoulders. His fair hair grew in tight wire springs close to his head. His features were heavy, but regular. He would have been quite good-looking if his face had had more life in it, but his eyes and mouth were frozen in a mould of tough impassivity, his favourite front to the world. His name was Macey—"King" Macey, he liked to be called. He was twenty-five.

The other looked puny beside him. His name was Chris Hines, and he was just twenty. He had a narrow head, flanked by enormous ears. Arched eye-brows and eyelids gave his face an expression of insolent surprise. He was wearing tight drainpipe trousers, pointed shoes, a black leather jacket with a fleece lining, and yellow knitted gloves. His dark hair was elaborately styled.

The older man wore a short camel-hair coat, suède shoes with thick crêpe soles, and brown leather gloves—an outfit deliberately chosen to mark his difference, his superiority, his leadership.

In the hazy pool of light Macey looked at his wrist-watch which he wore with the dial turned inwards like a commando's. The time was coming up to five minutes past nine. He waited, savouring the drama of the final seconds before zero hour.

"Okay," he said, "let's go."

Soft-footed and predatory, they crossed the deserted road to the Vauxhall. Macey opened the offside door and eased himself in behind the wheel. Hines walked round and slid into the seat beside him. Macey touched the starter and engaged second gear and let in the clutch, gently. He felt quite at home in the car—he'd stolen the same model before. Both men held the doors open until they were round the corner and could slam them in safety.

Getting out of the suburb took all Macey's concentration. He'd been over the route beforehand, memorising the turns, but in the murk the roads looked different.

"Fog's gettin' worse," Hines said.

Macey grunted.

"Think we'll be okay?"

"'Course we will . . ." Macey always sounded confident. "This fog's just the ticket. Make the getaway easy."

Hines's feet tapped nervously on the floorboard. Even when relaxed, he found it hard to keep still—and to-night he was on edge.

"Don't like fog," he said.

Macey gave him a contemptuous glance.

"Anyone'd think we was goin' to do a mail van. This'll be a piece o' cake—kid's stuff. . . ."

For a moment, Hines was silent. Then he nodded. "Guess you're right, King. . . ." He was an argumentative youth, but he rarely argued with Macey. Not because he had complete faith in his leader's judgment. Macey liked to behave as though he knew everything, as though he was God Almighty, but he *had* been in the nick a couple of times, which-wasn't so smart. Secretly, Hines thought he was pretty dim compared with himself. . . . Nor did he accept what his leader said because he was devoted to him. Macey always went on as though no one else mattered, and Hines resented that The simple fact was that he was afraid of Macey's strength.

2

Macey could break him in pieces if he wanted to. So he didn't argue too much. . . . Anyway, to be fair, things hadn't been going badly since he'd teamed up with Macey. Maybe the bloke was learning. They'd got away with that job in Hounslow, they'd got away with all the jobs they'd done on their way down to the West Country, They'd kept a jump ahead of the cops all the time—and they'd lived high. That was what appealed to Hines—the easy rewards of crime, the quick dough, the free spending. Comfort, clothes, girls, endless amusement. Hines was a hedonist. As long as Macey could deliver the goods, he'd go along with him. . . .

They were coming out of the suburb into the main road now, and the driving was easier. The patchy fog had thinned a little.

"There's the boozer," Macey said. Ahead, a wide forecourt opened out on the left with a pub sign over it. He braked to a stop and gave two light taps on the horn.

"There's Rosie," Hines said.

A girl came swiftly out of the gloom, with a click of high heels—a tinsel blonde, heavily made up, but pretty. She looked about seventeen. Even in her outdoor clothes she was very shapely, Hines opened the rear door for her and she climbed in.

"Thought you was never coming, darling," she said leaning forward and giving Macey a quick hug.

His head jerked irritably. "Don't see why—we're on time." The car moved off again, filled now with a cloying scent.

"P'raps I was early . . . I'm so excited, King, I can't tell you . . ." She sounded a bit breathless. "Can't really believe I'm coming with you."

Macey half turned. "Wrap up, Rosie, will you—we got work to do."

She subsided at once. She wasn't in the least submissive by nature—she'd always done exactly as she liked at home, she'd given constant trouble in the reform school, she was usually petulant and difficult with men—but she always did what Macey said. She'd been infatuated with him from the first moment she'd met him in that coffee bar on Brook Street two months ago—and she didn't mind who knew it. After all, it wasn't as though she couldn't pick and choose if she wanted to. All the boys had been after her, even before she'd won that beauty contest. Now she'd only have to lift a finger and they'd come flocking again. . . . But none of them was in King's class. None of them was as strong as King was, or as sure of himself. She adored King. She'd do anything for him. . . . She'd done most things. . . .

Macey drove on, frowning over the wheel. He wasn't sure he ought to have let Rosie come, she yapped too much—but he'd been keen for her to see just how well he did these jobs. She was a soft kid, too clinging, he'd probably be through with her pretty soon, but just now she was the queen in Salmouth all right and it gave him a warm feeling to be admired by a chick with a bit of form behind her. To be admired by anyone, come to that. . . .

The car cruised along slowly for another couple of hundred yards. They were approaching their destination now. Macey could feel the tenseness growing in Hines beside him. A blurred patch of light ahead sharpened into a neon sign—the Majestic Cinema. Macey stopped the car just short of the entrance. He'd picked the time well. It was the dead period, just after the start of the last picture, when no one was going in or coming out. A few pedestrians were passing in the street, but with long intervals between them. A few cars were going by, too, but their drivers were too busy peering through the fog to notice what was happening at a cinema. Everything was fine.

"Tommy's there," Hines said.

Macey nodded, A youthful figure was lounging outside the cinema, pretending to look at the advertisements of the film. Tommy Baker, aged seventeen, in drainpipe trousers and pointed shoes and a brown fleece-lined leather jacket. . . .

Macey said, "You know you gotta shift when we go, Rosie."

"Yes, King."

For a moment the occupants of the car sat motionless. The only sound was Rosie's quick breathing in the back. Baker was looking into the foyer of the cinema. . . . Suddenly he turned and raised his thumb.

Macey drove on a few yards and stopped outside the entrance.

"Okay," he said. Quickly, the two men tied handkerchiefs round the lower part of their faces. Rosie murmured, "Good luck, darling!" A rapid glance up and down the pavement—and they were out of the car and walking briskly into the cinema.

Except for the grey-haired woman behind the grille, the foyer was empty. Hines drew, a flick-knife from his jacket, shot the blade out, and stepped lightly through the door into the tiny box-office. The cashier was counting her takings, as she always did at that time. Hines's knife was at her throat before she could let out a sound. "One squeak an' I'll carve you," he said. He started to grab up the notes from the till and stuff them into his pocket. In the foyer, Macey was standing guard at the doors leading into the cinema. He had a gun in his hand. This was the moment he loved—the moment of power. He almost wished someone *would* come out, so he could show who was master. He was conscious of his own coolness, of his absolute command over himself. . . . All the same, he thought, Chris should be through by now. Five seconds passed, ten seconds. . . . A pedestrian went by in the street, without looking in. Macey called Out, "Get a move on, Chris!"

At that moment one of the cinema doors swung open. Macey jerked round—and the handkerchief slipped below his chin. A man had come out—a man in a dinner-jacket. The manager. . . . For a split second he stared at Macey, at the gun. His eyes swivelled to the box-office. Then he turned away. . . .

Macey levellad the gun and shot him at a yard's range. Plumb in the centre of his head, just above the left ear. . . . As he fell, someone screamed—the cashier. . . . Macey rushed for the pavement, with Hines on his heels. From nowhere, three people had somehow gathered in the street. Macey thrust a gaping woman out of his way and leapt into the back of the car. Hines, his face still covered, scrambled in at the other side. Tommy Baker was at the wheel, with Rosie beside him and the engine running. As he let in the clutch a man peered into the car, looking hard at Baker and Rosie. Then the Vauxhall roared away into the fog.

For seconds, no one said, a word. The shock waves in the dark car were almost palpable. Macey was the calmest. A leader had to be calm.

It was Rosie who found her voice first—a high, scared voice. "King—what happened?"

"He shot the bloody manager," Hines burst out. In his fear, he turned on Macey as he'd never done before. "You said no shootin', King."

"Aw, pipe down," Macey said. "The crazy bastard grabbed me arm an' the gun went off. How could I help it ...?" He'd have liked to tell the truth, to say the manager would have identified him and that was why he'd shot him, to boast of his first slaying—but it seemed unwise. These kids weren't ready for it.

"Let's get out o' here—we can yap later."

Baker turned, licking dry lips. "Where we makin' for, King?"

"Anywhere out o' town," Macey said. The plan had been for Rosie to go back home, and for the rest of them to lie up in their digs till the heat was off—but that wouldn't do now. They'd all been seen—and with a man shot, there'd be a big hue and cry. They'd got to keep moving. "Straight ahead, Tommy—an' step on it."

Rosie said, "Do you—is he—dead?"

"'Course he's dead. . . . Bullet went in over his ear-hole. Must have croaked before he hit the deck."

"You didn't mean to do it, though ..." Rosie was trembling. She'd come with them for kicks, but she'd never imagined anything like this. "It was an accident, King."

"'Course it was an accident."

The car swerved, as Baker narrowly but skilfully avoided the looming back of a lorry. He was driving well, concentrating on the few yards of road he could see, trying not to think about what had happened. He was proud of the trust Macey was putting in him, and eager to justify it. Baker wasn't afraid of Macey, the way Hines was, nor critical of him. Baker was a romantic and Macey was his heros—whatever he'd done.

A match scraped in the darkness. Hines's face, as he drew on the cigarette, had a desperate pallor. He kept turning to look back through the rear window, to see if they were being followed. When, presently, headlights showed through the gloom, he nearly shot off his seat.

"Cripes, ain't that a cop car on our tail?"

Macey swung round. "No—you just got the shivers, mate. . . ." But, in the murk, he wasn't quite sure. The car was coming on fast and gaining on them. "Better turn off, Tommy," he said. "Any place."

Almost at once Baker braked by a street lamp and swung the rocking car into a side turning. Rosie gasped and clutched the door handle.

"Keep goin'," Macey said, "We can easy work back to the main road later."

Baker kept going. The fog was thicker here—he could only just see the kerb.

Hines was sail gazing back through the rear window. The headlights had gone. "Reckon we lost him," he said in a tone of relief.

"Lost ourselves too." Baker said. The road had curved and forked and turned back on itself. They had entered a quiet residential area, without shops or signs or traffic.

Hines leaned forward. "Gotta keep goin' left, Tommy."

"Right, I reckon."

"You been turnin' right all the ruddy time," Hines said.

"Yeah, but the road twisted."

"It did twist," Rosie said.

"'Course it did, Rosie—but 'e took the right fork back there, see. . . Blimey, we goin' to mess around here till the cops find us?"

"Aw, turn it up," Macey said. "Keep right, Tommy."

"Sure, King." Baker drove on. Hines sat in anxious silence.

For a quarter of an hour they were hopelessly lost. The streets were empty, there was no one to give them directions. Rosie suggested calling at a house but Macey said it was too risky. Twice, with frustrated urgency, the futile argument broke out again. Then, as the fog suddenly lifted, they saw the lights of the main road ahead of them once more.

"See, I told you," Macey said. "Soon be out of it now."

Rosie put her hand over the back of the seat, feeling for his. "You was right, King. . . ." He acknowledged the tribute with a perfunctory squeeze of her fingers, then let them go. He preferred the feel of the gun in his pocket.

They were making good progress at last, doing nearly forty. In the wide main road the fog was just thick enough to give them good cover without impeding them. There was little traffic about. Two miles slipped by quickly. They'd soon be out of town now, Macey thought. With luck, they'd soon be out of the district. . . .

Suddenly Baker called out, "What's that in front, King?" A couple of hundred yards ahead there seemed to be lights all over the road. There were several stationary cars, and people walking about. . . .

"Accident?" Hines said, peering. Baker slowed.

"Blimey, it's a road block," Macey cried. "They've closed the bloody road . . .!"

Without waiting for orders, Baker swung the car round in a squealing U-turn and roared away in the direction from which they'd come. The fog engulfed them again. The lights behind them dimmed and faded.

"Good boy," Macey said softly.

"Cor, I thought we'd had it then. . . ." Hines groped for another cigarette with shaking fingers. "What we goin' to do now, King? Try another road?"

"If they've blocked one," Macey said, "reckon they'll have blocked 'em all. . . ."

"Perishin' fog!" Hines muttered, "It was losin' ourselves what did it."

"We can't just keep going round and round," Rosie wailed.

Macey was silent, trying desperately to think what to do. If they couldn't get out of town, they'd probably be better off on foot. The car wasn't going to any more use to them—and the cops would have its number by now. Better get rid of it. . . .

Ahead, the road divided. A sign on a lamp standard, pointing left, said, "To the Harbour."

"Left, Tommy," Macey said. "Be quieter that way."

Baker swung the wheel and drove on.

Hines said, "Maybe we oughter split up, King."

Macey stiffened. "Don't see how that'd help."

"Give us all a better chance."

Give the cops a better chance, you mean. . . . You want to split up, Rosie?"

"No, King—I want to stay with you."

"You want to split up, Tommy?"

"I'm stickin' with you, King."

"That's the boy," Macey said. His sudden, sharp fear that he might be left alone, without company, without lieutenants, subsided. "Okay, we stick together. . . ." He peered forward over Baker's shoulder. "Watch out for a dark turning, Tommy. We goin' to ditch the car."

They went on for fifty yards. Then Baker slowed. "This do, King?" On the left there was a tiny cul-de-sac. Macey said, "Yeah—fine." Baker turned the car in and switched off the lights.

"Right," Macey said, "all out"

Rosie picked up her bag. "Where we going, King?"

"Away from the car for a start. . . . Then I'll think o' something. . . ." They set off in a huddled group, keeping close to a low wall. The road was deserted. The fog swirled damply around them.

"We can't just go on walking," Rosie said. "Not all night. . . ." She stumbled as one of her heels caught in a broken bit of pavement. "It's awful here. . . ."

Macey jerked her forward impatiently, "Gotta keep movin'," he said. "Quit beefin', will you. . .?"

Suddenly they saw the lights of a car in the gloom ahead. Twin lights—and a third, a lighted panel above and between the others. Coming towards them. . . .

"Cops!" Hines said, and froze.

"Quick!" Macey cried. "Over the wall!"

They scrambled over. Baker helped Rosie. There was a stone jetty on the other side, and water, and a lot of small boats. Three or four deep they lay against the jetty—old cabin cruisers, most of them, laid up for the winter under tarpaulins. A nearby street lamp lit them with a hazy glow. A dangerous glow. . . .

"Come on!" Macey called. He climbed on to the nearest cruiser, and crossed it, and wriggled past ropes and obstructions to the boat on the outside. Its ancient tarpaulin was torn at a corner and he lifted it up and held it for the others. In a moment they were all crouching under cover.

"Listen!" Macey said.

They could hear the patrol car now. It was abreast of them, just over the wall. It was stopping. . . . They scarcely dared to breathe. . . . No, it was all right—it was just going slowly. . . . It was moving away. They hadn't been seen. . . .

The sound of the engine grew faint. Silence fell again. A silence broken, only by the wail of a ship's siren, far out at sea. . . .

"Cripes, that was a near one. . . ." Hines dug for a cigarette. "I made sure they seen us."

"Me too," Baker said.

"Fairies weren't half havin' a right game in me guts, I can tell you. . . ." Hines lit his cigarette, illuminating for a moment the circle of strained faces under the canvas.

"Good job you was quick, King," Baker said.

Macey shrugged. "Just gotta keep a cool head, Tommy."

"Any rate," Baker said, "we got a place to kip."

Rosie shivered. The boat stank of mildew and stale bilge water and every surface dripped. "We can't sleep here," she said. "We'll catch our death."

"It's better'n nothin', Rosie. . . . Good place to lie low, too."

"Blimey," Hines said, "you ain't suggestin' we stay here?"

"Why not . . .?"

"Use your nob, man—how we goin' to eat? Gotta eat, ain't we? First time we stick our bloomin' heads out, we're nicked."

"Not if it's dark. . . . Bet we could manage somehow."

"Well, this ain't no place to lie low, I can tell you that," Hines said. "They'd find us easy."

"I don't reckon no one comes here much, Chris.... Not this time o' year."

"The cops will," Hines said. "They'll, look every place. They'll comb the whole ruddy town till they find us."

"What we goin' to do, then?"

"I dunno," Hines said. "Reckon they got us in a trap, mate.... Ain't that right, King?"

Macey had been listening quietly to the argument. This was his method in a quandary—to listen, weighs, and finally pronounce. Thus he gained kudos without putting too much of a tax on his slow intelligence.... But this time the argument hadn't helped him. Chris was right—they *were* in a trap. The police must know they were still in the town and they'd go on searching till they found them. There was only one way to safety and that was, somehow, to break out of the ring.... But how ...?

Cautiously, he raised the corner of the canvas and looked out. Fog and silence lay over the yacht basin. Nothing stirred.

"Wonder if we could get away in this tub?" he said.

At once, Baker seized on the idea. "That's it, King.... Go up the coast a few miles an' land outside the town. That'd fox 'em."

"Land up the creek, more like," Hines said. "How'd we know we was goin' up the coast in this muck?"

"Well, it ain't goin' to last for ever, Chris.... What you say, Rosie?"

"'Course," Macey said, though he knew nothing. Neither did any of them.

"Bet you what you like it won't move."

"We can shove it out o' here," Baker said. "Make a start, any rate...."

Macey grunted. "Let's 'ave a dekko at it."

Baker unlaced the tarpaulin and rolled it back to the cabin top and they all stood up in the cockpit. The street lamp provided just enough light to see by. The cruiser was about thirty feet long with about ten feet of cockpit. By the look of it, it was a very old boat. The cabin door was locked but the lock broke away from the wood when Macey heaved on it. Inside there was a large saloon in a bad state of neglect. Macey struck a match and gazed around. The paint was peeling, the bunk cushions were green with mould. There were a few bits of gear lying about—old rope and cans and boxes and an anchor and a bucket—stuff that wouldn't come to much harm from being left. Otherwise, the boat had been stripped.

"There's a ladies', any rate," Rosie said, pushing open the door of a closet. They were all poking about now, their danger momentarily forgotten in the novelty of their surroundings. Hines, from the cockpit, said, "Go on, bet it's a gents'," and Rosie giggled, a bit hysterically. Hines was fiddling with the gear lever, the steering-wheel, the throttle—anything he could find that moved. Suddenly a raucous sound shattered the silence.

Macey looked out in alarm, "What was that?"

"Sorry, King," Hines said. "It's one o' them klaxons—put me ruddy arm on it.

"Well, watch it, man—you'll rouse the town. . . ."

Baker had lifted a wooden casing in the cockpit and was peering down with a lighted match, "Here's the engine," he said. "Diesel."

Hines scoffed. "How d'you know it's diesel?"

"Tell by the pong," Baker said. "Ain't like petrol. . . ." Baker, between bouts of delinquency, had once worked in a garage for a few weeks. He followed the fuel pipe with his hand, tracing it back to the tank in the stern locker. "Maybe there's some oil left in."

"'Ave a gander," Macey said.

Baker unscrewed the cap. Hines struck another match. "'Bout half full, King," Baker reported. He reached down and turned the tap on.

"You got a hope, mate," Hines said. "She won't never start."

Baker grasped the handle and tried to turn the engine over. It was a big engine and very stiff. All he could manage was a couple of slow revolutions. Nothing happened.

"Told you," Hines said.

Baker stood back, breathing hard. "Why don't you have a go?"

"Me?—not likely. Want me to rupture meself?"

Macey said, "Let me have a crack." He planted his feet firmly in front of the engine, gripped the handle in his great fist, and put all the power of his biceps and back into turning it. It went round easily now. Ten—a dozen revolutions. . . .

"Coo, he's strong," Rosie said.

Hines leered at her. "That's what you like, Rosie girl, ain't it . . .?"

Macey went on cranking. Finally, with a gasp, he had to give it up. Then, in the manner of diesels, the engine slowly came to life after he'd stopped turning.

"Blimey!" Hines said.

They hadn't expected it, they weren't ready for it. Now, suddenly, there was panic over the noise, the loud tack-tack, "We better clear out," Macey said. "Get them ropes untied." Hines and Baker started to fumble inexpertly with the lines. "Hurry!" Macey called. He was at the wheel, experimenting with the gear lever, revving the engine. Abruptly, the boat gave a lunge forward. The ancient head rope parted, then the stem rope. They were away! Scraping past the boat alongside them, sliding out into the basin, gathering speed. . . .

Macey peered ahead. "Can't see a ruddy thing," he cried. He groped for the throttle, which he'd temporarily lost. Before he could slow down, they hit something—hard. The boat shuddered to a stop. Baker climbed over the cabin top and looked down. They'd run slap into some heavy wooden piles. "Back up a bit, King," he called.

Macey found reverse and backed away from the piles and set off again at a slower pace. Almost at once they hit something else, some bit of staging, but only a glancing blow. They'd left the boats behind now. They seemed to be leaving the basin. Macey looked back. In spite of the engine row and all the shouting, they didn't appear to have roused anyone. There were no lights in the road, except the street lamps. No one was calling after them. The engine had settled down to a steady rhythm. All was well. . . .

"Reckon we made it," Macey said proudly. "Keep a good lookout there, Tommy. . . . Get that tarpaulin right off, Chris. . . ." He drew Rosie to him in a rough embrace. "Baby, am I glad to leave that town!"

They saw nothing of the harbour on their way out—nothing of any other ships afloat. Salmouth was a large and busy port, but to-night there seemed to be no one else on the move at all. The only sounds were the beat of their own engine and the occasional siren out at sea. "Guess they've all jacked it in," Macey said, with contempt for their lack of spirit. He felt fine at the wheel, in the stance of command. He had no serious worries—everything was under control. The weather was just what they needed. Not a breath of wind stirred the clammy blanket of fog. The water was calm—flat calm. The boat was gliding along as though on rails.

They had one close call, that shook Macey's confidence briefly. That was when they were well out of the harbour. Suddenly there was a shout from Baker and a tremendous banging and clattering along the cruiser's side. Something swished by with a light on top, flashing white. Even Baker hadn't seen the buoy until the last moment. Macey looked back, but already the iron monster had vanished. They must be going pretty fast.

Hines gave a cackle. "Better watch it, skipper!" Now that the tension of the land chase was over, he was feeling a bit light-headed.

Macey grunted and took a cigarette from his pocket. "Want a snout?"

"I'm burnin'."

"Gimme a touch, then."

Hines gave him a light from his own cigarette. The glowing tips were the only break in the blackness. Everywhere, everything, was dark—the cockpit, the cabin, the opaque night. Baker, up on the cabin top, was invisible.

Rosie said nervously, "Where we going, King?"

"Up the coast, like I said."

"Ain't you going away from it?"

"There's docks an' things," Macey said. "We gotta keep clear."

"When you goin' to turn then, King?" Hines asked.

"In a while, mate. . . . Gotta get away from the ruddy town first. . . . There's plenty o' time."

"How we goin' to get back on shore in the end?"

"Run her up on the beach somewhere, I reckon."

"Then we'll swipe another car, eh?"

"'Course. . . . Got the gilt safe, Chris?"

"You bet."

"How much?"

"I dunno. . . . 'Bout a hundred nicker."

"That'll do us—we'll be okay. . . . Bet the cops won't half be wonderin' what's happened to us."

"You been pretty smart, King," Baker said, from the cabin top.

"Gotta be, boy. . . . Gotta use your loaf. . . ." Macey gazed ahead into the darkness. "Have a butcher's at the oil, Tommy, will you?"

Baker climbed down and inspected the tank by matchlight. "Okay," he said. "Still pretty near half."

"Don't use much, does she . . .?" Macey was silent for a while, thinking about when he'd better turn. The trouble was, he didn't know which direction they'd been coming in. Not exactly. He'd tried to point the boat straight out when they'd left the harbour and he'd kept the wheel steady ever since—but that might not mean a lot. It was going to be tricky. If he turned too soon, or too much, they might finish up back in Salmouth. . . . But if he left it too late, there might not be enough oil to reach the land. . . . No hurry yet, though. They'd only been going half an hour. . . .

Rosie said, "I ain't half cold, King."

"Why don't you go an' lay down inside then . . .? Bet it's warmer in there."

"Think I will," Rosie said, She went into the cabin.

For another quarter of an hour Macey kept the cruiser going without changing direction. The sea around them was as smooth as a lake. The fog was thinning a little, but the ships' sirens were still warning and answering each other out in the Channel. There was a new noise, too—a very loud, deep noise, that sounded regularly every few minutes and ended in a giant's grunt.

"What the hell's that?" Macey said.

Hines shrugged in the darkness, "Search me, mate. . . . Ship, I s'pose."

"That ain't no ship. . . . It ain't movin'."

"There's a lighthouse out 'ere somewhere," Baker said. "Saw a pitcher of it on the pier. Swirlstone, they call it."

Hines gazed around. "I can't see no light."

"'Course you can't," Baker said, "'cos o' the fog. That's why there's a fog signal."

"Bloody row, any rate," Hines muttered. He stamped his feet, trying to warm them. "Cor, I reckon we come miles. . . . What's the time, Tommy?"

Baker struck a match. "Quarter past one."

"'Struth! Wish I 'ad some grub. . . . Ain't you goin' to turn, King?"

"Any minute now," Macey said.

"We'll be in ruddy France soon. . . . Hope you know where you're goin'."

"Over there," Baker said, pointing.

"Don't be daft, Tommy. . . . That's where we come from."

The fog signal sounded again, much nearer. But now it seemed to come from a different direction.

"Reckon we're goin' round in flippin' circles," Hines said.

At that moment there was an agitated cry from the cabin. Rosie shot out, stumbling over the entrance in her excitement. "The water's coming in, King. . . . It's all over the floor."

Baker struck a match and held it up in the doorway. "It is too!" He said in a startled voice. The floor-boards were covered. "Must 'ave spring a leak, king."

Hines looked over Baker's shoulder. "I bet we done it when we hit them posts."

"Go on, she's just an old tub," Macey said. "Here, take over, Chris. . . ." He gave the helm to Hines and joined Baker at the cabin door.

"Wish we'd got a torch," Baker said. He struck another match.

Macey looked at the water in dismay. "Pretty bad, ain't it?"

"Maybe there's a pump somewhere. . . ." Baker started to grope around in the cockpit. Presently he found one. It was a semi-rotary, fixed to a bulkhead. But when he tried to work the handle it wouldn't budge. "Reckon it's rusted up, King."

"Okay, we'll have to make do with the bucket."

Baker slopped through the cabin and fetched it Macey prised up a couple of floorboards and took the bucket and started to bail. The water was perceptibly higher than when he'd first seen it.

Bailing wasn't easy. It had to be done in darkness, to husband their dwindling store of matches. Each bucketful of water had to be passed out through the narrow doorway and emptied overboard Macey and Baker were soon sweating freely. They bailed hard for five minutes. Then Baker struck another match. They seemed to be holding their own, but no more.

Macey dashed the sweat from his eyes. "Here, you come an' have a go, Chris. . . ." Hines left the wheel and took the bucket. Macey went and put the gear lever an neutral and throttled the engine down. This job was going to need all hands.

It was very quiet with the engine shut down—except when the fog signal boomed. That was beginning to sound very close.

Hines was fresh, and at first he bailed furiously—but he flagged more quickly than the others. Presently Baker relieved him in the cabin and Hines shot the water overboard. Then Macey took over from Baker. Turn and turn about, they bailed away. Gradually, the operation began to slow down. They were all getting tired. . . . When they slowed, the water rose at once.

"Reckon it's got worse," Baker said, breathing hard.

Rosie clutched Macey's arm in sudden panic. "King, we ain't going to sink, are we?"

"'Course we ain't," Macey said.

Hines struck a match. The water was almost level with the cockpit floor now. "Cor!" he said, staring. "What we goin' to do, King?"

"Keep bailin'," Macey said. Baker picked up the bucket. Macey gazed around, into the fog.

Baker said, "What about headin' full speed for the shore, King?"

"That's just it, boy," Macey said slowly. "Where *is* the bloody shore?"

They looked round together, in appalled silence. The boat had been left to itself while they'd been bailing. It had swung and it had drifted. No one now had even the slightest sense of direction.

"No good makin' for the shore if we don't know where it is," Macey said.

Baker was frantically scooping up water again. It was a simpler operation now—he could do it from the cockpit. But he made little impression, "Reckon we *will* sink," he gasped.

Rosie let out a wail. "King—what are we going to do?"

The fog signal went off again. It was somewhere on their right, close enough to startle them.

Baker suddenly jerked upright. "Why don't we make for the lighthouse. King. . . .? Reckon it's our only chance."

"Just what I was thinking boy," Macey said—though it hadn't occurred to him. He went to the wheel and thrust the gear in and throttled up. No one argued—not even Hines. Any alternative seemed better than sinking and drowning.

"Keep bailing!" Macey shouted. "Don't, want the engine to conk. . . ." The propeller shaft was sending up fountains of water. "Bail for your ruddy lives!"

Baker and Hines applied themselves to the bucket with new energy. Macey steered in what he thought was the direction from which the last signal had sounded. Rosie stood beside him in the slopping water, gazing ahead.

The signal went off again, a little to the right still, shatteringly close. Macey turned the wheel a fraction.

Suddenly Rosie cried, "I can see a light. King!"

"Where?"

"Straight in front. . . . Now it's gone."

Macey peered into the darkness. In a moment, a hazy glow appeared right in their track, a shrouded cluster of beams, that revolved and disappeared and showed again.

"We're nearly there," Macey yelled to the bailers. "Keep at it, mates!"

The light grew steadily brighter, Macey throttled the engine down. It wasn't easy to judge distance in the fog, but they must be very close. He wondered if they'd be able to go right up to the lighthouse door and step out. The sea was calm enough. . . .

Then with a grinding crash, the boat hit something and shuddered to a stop.

"Blimey, what's 'appened?" Hines cried.

"Reckon we struck a rock," Baker said.

Macey switched off the engine and they all crowded to the side. They couldn't see any rock—only water all round them, necked with white. They were still some way from the lighthouse—thirty yards, maybe. They could just make out the vague shape of the tower, rising eerily in the fog.

They felt no sense of relief yet. The boat was making horrible noises under them. The water looked deep and cold. They'd almost reached the lighthouse but they couldn't see any way of getting to it. . . .

The fog signal went off, practically overhead, almost deafening them with its blast and its grunt.

Baker was looking over the side. Presently he said.

"Reckon the tide's goin' down. King. . . . Boat ain't makin' such a row now."

It was true. The cruiser was beginning to settle. The jarring and scraping wasn't nearly so bad.

"Shan't float off, any rate," Baker said.

Rosie was still scared. "What we going to do, King?"

"Better start shoutin'," Macey said.

They all shouted. Hines shouted and worked the klaxon too. They shouted until they were hoarse. But nothing happened.

"Don't believe they'll ever hear us," Rosie whimpered.

"'Course they will," Macey said. "Bound to, some time. . . . Then they'll come an' help us."

"What we goin' to do when we get in there?" Hines asked.

"Don't you worry about that, mate," Macey said, "Just leave it to me."

Chapter Two

High up in the Swirlstone Tower, the principal keeper, George Robeson, was on watch. He had taken over at midnight and would be on duty until four.

Robeson was a veteran of the lighthouse service. Almost forty-five years had passed since he'd signed on as a young supernumerary, and now, with his sixty-fifth birthday approaching, he was soon to retire. His appearance and manner perfectly matched his record. He was a solid, burly man, with a weatherbeaten face and close-cropped grey hair. His blue eyes, deep-set under grizzled brows, were serene and wise. The crowsfeet that fanned from their corners gave him a look of tolerance and humour. The overall impression was of calm and sure authority, born of vast experience, modestly worn, and quietly exercised. And this was right.

He was keeping his watch in the service room—the operational and administrative hub of the lighthouse, conveniently placed below the lantern. It was here that all the records were kept, the weather reports made out, the log book brought up to date. Here too, were most of the meteorological instruments—the barometer, the thermometer, the wind-force indicator. There was a small table to work at, and a chair, and on another table the VHF radio-telephone set that was used for all communication with the shore. The room was round, like all the rooms in the tower; spotlessly clean, with aseptic whitewashed walls, and very small. The diameter, not counting the considerable cupboard space, was hardly more than twelve feet.

Robeson was sitting back in the chair, comfortable in the blue jersey that he preferred to his formal jacket, puffing at his pipe and reading one of the newspapers that his assistant, Mitchell, had brought back on the relief boat the previous day. He looked and felt relaxed, for at this hour there was little for him to do except keep an eye and an ear open. Through the window he could see the glow of the revolving light against the wall of fog. From far down in the tower came the low, steady hum of the generator. There was nothing to give him any concern.

Recently, the Swirlstone had gone over from oil to electricity, and the nearly "push-button" system of control had taken most of the heavy work and anxiety out of the night watch. There was no need any longer to wind once an hour the clockwork mechanism that in the old days had revolved the light. There was no need to watch and tend a lamp. Now almost everything was automatic. If, in the lantern room above, the electric bulb should fail, another would swing instantly into place and a warning light would show on an indicator panel until the defective bulb was changed. If anything should go wrong with the mechanism that turned the optic, a different light would show. If, down in the engine room, the generator should develop any fault, an alarm would ring—and there were two spare generators, either of which could be switched on in a second. Robeson, a man old in years but not in outlook, approved the new arrangements. When it had been necessary, he had wound up weights and trimmed wicks with devotion and pleasure. Lighthouse work had been a bondage then, but he'd always loved it. He'd enjoyed even the dullest routine because in some way it had served the light, and serving the light had been his vocation and his pride. He'd chosen the life, quite simply, because he'd wanted to be of use in the world—and keeping ships away from the rocks was a useful job, a job that warmed his heart. . . . All the same, after nearly half a century of hard, slogging work in lighthouses of every kind around the coast, he was all for avoiding pointless chores. There were still plenty of the other sort. . . .

The fog signal boomed. The noise was muted a little by the tower's granite walls, which even at this height were more than two feet thick, but it was still loud enough to set the air vibrating. Robeson put the paper aside, the thread of his reading broken. He was a reflective man, and for a while he sat contentedly smoking and thinking. He thought about the previous day's relief and, thankfully, how well it had gone. It was always a matter for satisfaction when a relief had been safely accomplished—the returning man landed, the departing one transferred, the stores hauled up. These monthly change-overs were tricky and hazardous even when the weather was reasonably good—and of course you never knew for certain that they would take place. Robeson could remember many occasions when the weather had been quiet almost to the last moment, and then had suddenly deteriorated. That meant that the man who was going ashore had to unpack all his gear again, and everyone became fretful and impatient and on edge. And you could never tell how long bad weather was going to last. Robeson had once spent four months in a rock tower, unrelieved—though admittedly that had been in the days of pulling boats, when it took four strong men to row close in.... But once the relief was completed, everyone felt fine. You could settle down, then, for another month: and of course there were letters and newspapers and books, brought by the man who'd returned, and gossip from the outside world, not to mention fresh meat and vegetables for a few days.... Yes, there was nothing like a successful relief....

A shadow crossed Robeson's face. He wouldn't know many more reliefs now. He felt sad about that. He felt sad, too, because his wife had died a year ago, because his family was grown-up and scattered, because when he went ashore for the last time, he'd be alone. He knew he'd miss the close, loyal companion-ship of the tower. Retirement was going to take a bit of getting used to. But he was only a little sad. He and Jane had had a long, happy time together, even if for years and end he had only seen her for one month out of four. Those months had been good months.... He'd had a fine life, taken all round—better than most. And he was still sound in mind and body. Old age would have its satisfactions. He'd find something to do.... Robeson had a common-sense, homespun philosophy that usually carried him through....

His last month or two, he thought, should be pleasant ones. He liked all his assistants—Granger, who was on leave, and Mitchell—even if Mitchell did have a bit of a chip on his shoulder—and certainly the new young fellow, Jim Lowe. A most promising lad—willing, tactful, anxious to learn. A lad with some depth in him, too, Robeson guessed—he should go a long way in the service. Very quiet and intelligent. A listener and a watcher—that was Lowe. And a remarkably good cook—which meant a great deal in the tower. Baked almost as good bread as Robeson did himself . . .!

The fog signal boomed again. A horrible noise, Robeson thought, matching the horrible night. . . . He hated fog—like all light-keepers. It made more work, and the constant blast of the siren was disturbing. You never quite got used to it. . . . Still, the weather should have improved by the morning. . . .

Assistant Keeper Mitchell was pacing to and fro on the floor, above. His feelings about the fog were similar to Robeson's, but sharper—for he was on fog watch. If the night had been clear it would have been his watch below and he'd have been asleep in his bunk. Instead, he was doing eight hours in a row. Still, it was all part of the job. . . .

Mitchell was a lean, active man of forty. He had a long, fine nose, a pointed chin, and slight hollows under his cheekbones. His head, with its sleek hair receding from a widow's peak, had a streamlined look. His mouth was thin and a trifle sardonic. He wasn't handsome, but he was quite striking. Though he lacked Robeson's thickset strength, he was muscular and wiry. He gave the impression of great alertness and competence.

Apart from a couple of seasons in a fishing boat in his youth, Mitchell, like Robeson, had spent the whole of his working life in the lighthouse service, and like Robeson he'd never regretted it. But his approach to the service was very different from the principal keeper's. It had a strong negative element, a tinge of bitterness. Mitchell was no selflessly dedicated man, eager to serve humanity. On the contrary, he was something of a misanthrope as far as the mass of the human race was concerned. He hated life ashore, especially modern, urban life. He loathed the rush and noise, the shoving and jostling, the cars and the fumes, the feeling of conflict never far away. To him, the tower was an escape, a retreat from the hostile land into blessed seclusion. If he hadn't been obliged to, he would rarely have taken his shore leave at all. Ashore, he was a misfit—a jaundiced spectator of the roaring struggle, given to sharp-tongued comment on every-thing he disliked. Naturally, he had few friends.

It might have been different, he knew, if he'd married, if he'd found the right sort of girl, as Robeson had. That might have reconciled him to the month-in-four ashore; it might have softened and mellowed him. He wished it could have happened. But the girl he'd been set on marrying, a Plymouth girl, had let him down and gone off with some slicker from London, some wide boy with money. She hadn't even said good-bye. He'd never forgiven her—and ashore, where wide boys proliferated, he could never forget the souring incident. . . . On the rock, he was a different man—cheerful, companionable, salty of humour, but never sharp, always full of some new interest. And in every way he was an able and conscientious keeper.

He was in the lantern room now moving around with a quiet, irregular tread—the tread of a busy, watchful man, not of a caged one. From time to time he went out on to the open gallery to see if there was any sign of a clearance and listen to the distant sirens—but it was dank and cold outside, even with his reefer jacket over his jersey, and the blasts from the diaphone were deafening. Inside, it was much pleasanter.

The lantern room was large by the standards of the tower—fourteen feet in diameter and nearly twenty to the cupola that formed its roof. Its circular wall consisted entirely of large, diamond-shaped panes of glass. Exactly in the centre stood an iron staging, six feet high, with a fenced, circular platform on top, reached by a short metal ladder. Above the platform rose the light cage—a neat, three-foot optic with a thousand prisms, revolving almost silently on rollers of polished steel, magically transforming a single electric bulb of little more than a thousand watts into six pairs of light beams, equidistantly spaced, of more than half a million candle power and with a staggering visual range. Precision, efficiency and beauty could hardly go further.

At the moment, though, the light was of minor importance. It had to shine and revolve, even though no one could see it—but the vital job was to look after the fog signal. . . . Not that the signal required a great deal of attention. Mitchell had already checked the character machine that timed the compressed air blasts and loosed the uproar once every five minutes. From time to time he went to look at the compressor, just to make sure that everything was working properly. But he expected no trouble. All the machinery in the Swirlstone, like the tower itself, was kept in meticulous order by keepers who had an equal pride in it. With ordinary luck, there'd be nothing but overseeing to do until, in due course, someone stepped over to the switchgear that controlled both the siren and the light, and pressed a few buttons.

Whistling a cheerful tune, Mitchell continued to prowl around. It felt good to be back in the tower. A little strange, maybe, after his month of enforced absence—but that was quite normal. The rooms always seemed small, the walls confining, to the returned keeper for the first day or so. The feeling would soon wear off. For Mitchell, the tower was home. . . .

Jim Lowe was lying on his bunk in the bedroom, which was one floor down from the service room. For the past couple of hours he'd been trying to sleep, but the fog signal had been so disturbing that all he'd managed to do was doze. Now he'd finally given up the struggle and was lying awake, re-reading a newsy letter that the relief boat had brought from the shore. It was from his father, who was the coxswain of the Salmouth lifeboat, and it gave an exciting account of a recent trip to a steamer that had broken in half.

Lowe was a big, broad-shouldered young man of twenty-one, with an open, rather chubby face on which life had so far etched no lines. His hair was thick and straw-coloured, a bit of a mop. His eyes were dark brown, large and fine, with a gentle, contemplative expression. His mouth was sensitive. In general, he took much more after his mother than his rugged father. He was an imaginative and studious youth, a great reader of books. He had benefited greatly from his grammar school education— something that his father had never been offered.

He had been in the lighthouse service for only a year and a half, but in that time he'd covered a good deal of ground and revealed considerable aptitude for the job. Though rather deliberate, even slow, in his physical movements, he'd quickly mastered the technical aspects of his training, showing a curiosity and interest which went well beyond the call of duty. He was competent now to manage lanterns, maintain burners, make minor repairs to machinery, signal with flags, use most kinds of radio installation, operate fog signals and the various controls of an electric station, cook a good meal for three, and give first aid. He had gained, his practical experience as a supernumerary, helping out at any lighthouse where, because of sickness or special leave, there was a temporary gap to be filled. Altogether he had served periods in eight rock lighthouses, and four shore stations. Now, at an unusually early age, he was doing his first job as a fully-fledged assistant keeper modestly and well.

The thing that had brought Lowe into the lighthouse service was a passionate love of the sea. As a boy he had talked of actually going to sea, but the sight of the Swirlstone from his father's fishing boat one day had so caught his imagination that he'd decided there and then to become a keeper. And the job had perfectly suited his temperament. He found in the great ocean a poetic mystery which deeply appealed to him. He loved the sense of space, the wide skies, the music of the waves. He loved the awe-inspiring grandeur of wild weather. He enjoyed the isolation, so different from loneliness. There was nothing negative about his attitude, as there was about Mitchell's—nothing he was running away from. Nor was he self-consciously aware of lofty motives, of the service he was doing. He simply happened to be an unusually self-contained, deeply contented young man with a liking for Nature in the raw, and at present he was finding absolute fulfilment in the tower. . . .

The fog signal blasted again. Lowe finished his letter and took a book from the rack above his head. It would soon be time for him to go on watch—he might just as well read for the rest of his spell below. He was soon absorbed in an account of a single-handed crossing of the North Atlantic in a twenty-foot sloop. . . .

At about half past two, Robeson left the service room to take a look at the weather outside. With the unhurried step of a man who knew that everything around him was in perfect order, he climbed to the lantern. Mitchell was squatting on the bottom rung of the optic ladder, his nose in a paperback. He looked up as the principal keeper's head appeared. "Still pretty thick, Rob. . . ."

Robeson nodded. "Glad I'm not out there in the Channel. . . ." He went through the door on to the gallery and leaned over the waist-high railing. The fog seemed to him a little less dense, but it still presented an impenetrable wall to the light beams. He stood for a moment, sniffing the wet air and listening. Several sirens were wailing—but all were a long way off. Vessels would be giving the rock a wide berth on a night like this. The hundred and fifty feet below, was invisible and silent. Robeson had never known it in a quieter mood—not at the Swirlstone. . . .

Suddenly, his attention was caught. There was a noise from below—a raucous noise that he couldn't place. He listened, one ear bent, trying to identify it. It was definitely outside the tower. . . . For a second or two it was drowned by the blare of the diaphone. Then, as the giant's grunt died away, he heard it again. And something more—the unmistakable cries of human voices. Voices crying "*Help . . .!*"

He went quickly into the lantern room. "Mitch!—there's someone down on the ridge."

Mitchell stared at him incredulously. "Can't be."

"There is, I tell you. . . . Must be a boat aground."

Mitchell went out and listened. "Good God!" he said.

"Come on down. . . ."

Robeson led the way, stopping at the bedroom to call out Lowe. The situation was unprecedented, but after the first burst of excitement they went calmly about their preparations. All three donned thigh boots and the life-jackets that were compulsory for any keeper going outside the tower. Mitchell and Lowe equipped themselves with torches and Robeson hung a loud hailer round his neck. Then they quickly descended the staircase. No one spoke on the way down. Robeson and Mitchell were pondering the state of the tide, the problems of approach and rescue. Lowe sensed their preoccupation.

They reached the entrance room. Lowe unfastened the stay bars and drew the bolts of the double entrance doors—made of gunmetal and weighing nearly half a ton each—and swung them back on their oiled hinges. Mitchell took a coil of rope from a hook and draped it over his shoulder. Outside the doors there was a vertical gunmetal ladder fixed to the granite of the tower, with twenty-three rungs a foot apart. They descended rapidly to the "set-off"—a five-foot-wide stone ledge with a fence round it that encircled the base of the lighthouse. From there, a shorter vertical ladder took them down to the rock on which the tower was built.

Cries were still coming across the narrow stretch of water. Lowe and Mitchell shone their torches in the direction of the sound. At first they could make out nothing but a vague shadow in a dazzling halo. Then, as the fog swirled and momentarily thinned, they saw with astonishment the shape of the stranded cruiser, leaning over now at a sharp angle, and the figures of the three men and the girl, waving and shouting from the cockpit. One of them seemed about to climb out, until Robeson called through the loud hailer, "We're coming—stay where you are."

The ridge of rock that ran unbroken between the boat and the lighthouse was still under water in places, but by Robeson's calculations there couldn't be more than a foot of it. He took the rope from Mitchell, tied one end to an iron ring in the tower wall, and waded out towards the cruiser, in the light of the torches, paying out the line behind him. The going was treacherous over the uneven, weed-covered rock but he took his time, planting his feet firmly, and reached the boat without mishap. There he made the rope fast, so that it would serve as a lifeline, and called the others over.

The keepers wasted little time on inspection of the shivering, bedraggled figures in the cockpit—and even less on conversation. Almost the only words spoken were Robeson's quiet instructions. Lowe climbed aboard and handed out the girl, lifting her as easily as though she'd been a small child. Mitchell showed her the lifeline and told her to hang on to it and supported her through the water to the foot of the tower. The three young men followed, helped at every step by one or other of the keepers. When they were safe, Lowe brought the rope in.

There was still the problem of getting the survivors up to the entrance door. They were wet and numbed and clearly in no condition to climb vertical ladders in the dark, unaided. The long ladder, especially, would be most dangerous—a fall from the top could easily be fatal. Robeson spoke to Lowe. "Better use the winch, Jim. . . ." Lowe nodded, and went quickly up the tower to the winch room and opened the doors and lowered a stout rope past the entrance door to the rock. Mitchell tied a bowline round the girl and encouraged her, as the winch gently took the strain. That way, she managed both ladders without difficulty. When she was safely at the entrance door, the others were roped and hauled up in turn. Mitchell collected the torches and loud hailer and coiled his line, and put it back on its hook. Robeson secured the doors. "Up you go," he said. "You're all right now."

The weary group made heavy work of the ascent—particularly the girl. The staircase, cunningly set into the thickness of the wall so that each room remained a closed and separate entity behind its door, was a very steep iron spiral. Outside each door there was a small landing, and several times the party stopped to rest before plodding on. It was with sighs of relief that they finally followed Lowe into the living-room of the tower, three floors from the top.

They made quite a crowd when they were all in. The room was only fourteen feet in diameter and a lot of the space was already taken up. There was a modern range, with, a small oven and a glowing coal fire. Beside it there was a sink, with a tank overhead for fresh water. There was also a. dresser, a pantry, cupboards and lockers; and in the centre of the room around table and three chairs. With seven people in there as well, three of them large men, there was hardly an inch to spare.

For the moment, Robeson gave the soaked and shivering survivors no more than, a collective glance. Any talking would clearly have to wait until they'd recovered a little. "Better make some tea, Jim," he said. "They'll want something to eat, too—they look famished. . . ." Lowe nodded, and started to take down crockery and put food on the table. The kettle was already singing on the stove. Mitchell poked the coal into a blaze.

"You sit here by the fire, girl," Robeson said, pulling up a chair for Rosie. "You'll soon dry. . . . You two take those other chairs. . . ." Obediently, Hines and Baker sat down. There was a bit more room now. Macey stood by the wall, hands in pockets, his face expressionless.

The meal was soon ready, Lowe poured mugs of tea and passed them round. "Help yourselves to grub," Robeson said. There was shore bread, still fresh in its polythene bag, and butter, and ham, and tomatoes, and cheese. The quartet needed no second invitation and tucked in ravenously. Their clothes were beginning to steam in the warm room.

While they ate, Robeson scrutinised them. A funny-looking lot, he thought—and they were certainly in a mess. Especially, the girl, with black stains on her cheeks from the stuff she'd put on her eyelashes. . . . But at least a little life was coming back into their faces now. It was time to hear their story.

The fog signal went off, Robeson waited for the noise to die. Then he said "You kids must be out of your minds. . . . What on earth were you doing out in a boat on a night like this?" He looked around for the spokesman.

"We was takin' a trip round the harbour, that's all," Macey said. "Salmouth. . . . Bit of a lark, see . . .? Then we lost ourselves an' the ruddy boat started to leak. Couldn't do nothin' about it so we come here. . . . We been shoutin' for half an hour."

Robeson grunted. He didn't like Macey's tone—or the look of him. Or the look of any of them, for that matter. Mitchell was eyeing them with even greater I distaste.

"Whose boat is it?" Robeson asked. None of them looked to him like a boar owner.

"It's my boat," Macey said. "Had it for years."

"What's her name?"

Macey hesitated. "*Rose*," he said.

Robeson shook his head. "The name on her bows is *Heron*. . . . You stole her, didn't you?"

"'Course not," Macey said. Then he shrugged. "If you must know, we borrowed her. . . . That's right, Chris, ain't it? Just for a bit of a trip, like. We was goin' to put her back when we done with her—so what's the fuss?"

"It's a miracle you weren't all drowned."

"Not much loss either, if you ask me," Mitchell said.

With a sigh, Robeson turned towards the door.

"What you goin' to do?" Macey asked.

"What do you think I'm going to do?" Robeson said. "Call up the shore and report you, of course."

"What's the hurry?"

"I want you off before the weather changes—it's going to be difficult enough having you here for one night. . . . I'd better have yout names."

"Sure," Macey said. He shot a warning glance at Hines and Baker, who got to their feet. "That's Chris Hines, that's Tommy Baker, that's Rosie—an' I'm Macey. 'King' Macey . . ."

Suddenly, the gun was out. "Just stand away from that door, feller, if you want to live. This gun's loaded—an' I ain't kiddin'."

There was a moment of incredulous silence. The keepers all stared at the gun. It was pointing straight at Robeson's chest. The hand that held it was steady; the eyes behind it were like grey pebbles. Robeson stood as though transfixed. This was a situation he had no idea how to cope with.

It was Mitchell who reacted first. "Why, you bloody young thug ..." he cried, and started across the room.

Hines intercepted him, his flick-knife bared. "Lookin' for trouble, bright boy?"

"You make another move like that," Macey said "an' I'll shoot you dead."

"You wouldn't dare ..." Mitchell's face had turned purple with anger.

"Like to bet, feller ...? I done in one bloke tonight already—second one ain't goin' to make no difference."

"He didn't mean to him," Rosie said.

"Belt up, Rosie, I'll do the talkin'.... So I ain't got nothin' to lose, see? Get that, will you—nothin' to lose! I'll do every last one o' you if I got to—soon as look at you...."

Robeson's eyes were on Rosie. Macey, he thought, could have been bluffing about a killing—but the girl looked frightened enough to be telling the truth. "Better take it easy, Mitch.... I think he means it."

Mitchell dropped his arms in a helpless gesture.

"That's more like it," Macey said. "Right, let's get organised. ..." He surveyed his troops. "Tommy, you go an' find some rope an' we'll tie these geezers up...." Baker went off with alacrity.

Robeson said, "You don't imagine you'll get away with this, do you?"

"Gettin' away with it now, ain't I ...?" Macey took a piece of ham from the table, inspected it, and popped it into his mouth. He felt very cool, very much in control. The gun had cowed the keepers, as it always cowed everyone. With the gun out, he felt sure of himself. He lolled back against the wall. "How you doin', Rosie? Dryin' out?"

"I'm all right," she said. She was so scared, her voice was hardly audible. She kept casting apprehensive glances at Hines's knifes which she hadn't seen before.

There was a step on the stair and Baker came in with a coil of thin rope. "How's this, King?"

"Just the job," Macey said. "Cut it up into bits—six bits....

'Bout that long." He demonstrated, without taking his eye off the keepers.

Baker hacked up the rope with the breadknife.

"Okay," Macey said. With the gun, he motioned to Mitchell to move nearer to Robeson, so that he could cover them both at once. "Now tie the kid up, Tommy." The kid was evidently Lowe, who hadn't spoken. "You stand over 'im, Chris. . . . Wrists an' ankles. Better get him on the floor first."

Hines pointed Hs knife at Lowe. "Down you go." Lowe glanced at Robeson. Robeson gave a grim nod. Lowe sat down with his back to the wall. Baker tied his feet together and his hands behind his back. Mitchell watched the knots. They were landsman's knots. They wouldn't be easy to get undone.

"Now you." Macey jerked the gun at Mitchell.

Mitchell glared at him. "You'll pay for this . . ."

"Down on the floor, big mouth."

Mitchell sat down and allowed himself to be tied. Robeson followed him. Now the three keepers were secured in a row against the wall. Hines clicked his knife back into its sheath.

Macey looked around complacently, "Well, we captured their bleedin' castle all right."

"An' not a shot fired," Hines said, with a cackle. "That was good, King . . . eh, Rosie?"

"S'pose so," Rosie said. She felt relieved that no one else had got hurt.

Macey drew up one of the chairs and sat down on it, his arms resting on the back. "Right—now we're goin' to have a little yap. . . . You—what's your name? You what was goin' to start a bundle."

"Mitchell."

"Okay, Mitchell—talk. How far to the shore from 'ere?"

Mitchell didn't answer.

"You better talk, feller, if you know what's good for you." Macey jerked the gun.

'I'll tell you . . ." Robeson began anxiously.

"You keep your trap shut," Macey said. "This geezer's gotta learn. . . . Put the frighteners on 'im, Chris."

Hines felt for his knife. Then he paused. . . . With an evil grin, he took from the table the polythene bag that the bread had been wrapped in and jammed it down over Mitchell's head. "If he ain't goin' to talk, he don't need no air."

"That's right," Macey said.

Behind the transparent bag, Mitchell's face grew slowly darker and redder. His mouth fell open, his eyes began to pop. His feet and hands strained at their ropes. He was gasping. . . . Baker watched with growing horror, Robeson shouted, "Take it off—you'll kill him." Rosie joined in. "King—oh, King, take it off . . . *Please!*"

With a regal gesture, Macey motioned to Hines. Hines whipped the bag off. Mitchell's breath rasped painfully as he drew long lungfuls of air. It was a full minute before his face returned to its normal colour.

"Okay," Macey said. "Now you've had your lesson, maybe you'll talk. . . . How far to the shore?"

"It's twelve miles to Salmouth . . ." Mitchell was still panting. "Eight to the nearest bit of coast."

"What bit's that?"

"It's called Sheep Head."

Macey nodded. "An' when's our boat goin' to float?"

Mitchell looked questioningly at Robeson, Robeson said, "I shouldn't think it'll ever float—not after grounding on those rocks. . . . Anyway, I thought you said it leaked already."

"Leak can be fixed, can't it . . .? When will it float if it's fixed?"

Robeson, considered for a moment. "About two in the afternoon, if the weather keeps like this."

"You any good at fixin' leaks, Mitchell?"

"I might be," Mitchell said. "Depends on the leak."

"You better be . . .! Soon as it's light, you can start."

Hines said, "What's the plan, then, King?"

"Float off an' make for the shore, o' course. . . . Then beat it."

"What about the fog? What about findin' the way?"

"Don't reckon the fog'll be so bad to-morrer," Macey said, "Never is in the daytime," He spoke as though the subject was closed. "Rosie, you better get some kip—if that bloody row up top don't stop you.... You too, Tommy—only got an hour or two. Find where these geezers kip an' help yourselves."

Rosie got up, "Where's the ladies'?"

"There's a place down in the entrance room," Robeson said.

Macey nodded. "Show her, Tommy."

Hines winked at Baker. "See you behave yourself, mate."

Baker said, "Come on, Rosie, let's go an' have a doss...." Rosie picked up her bag and they went off down the spiral.

Hines gave a big yawn. What with the car chase, and the boat, and the anxious moments in the tower, he felt tired out. "What we goin' to do, King?"

"We goin' to watch these geezers, boy. Take it in turns, see. You get yourself a bit o' shut-eye now, an' I'll wake you in an hour. ..."

"Okay," Hines said. He put two of the chairs together and stretched out before the fire with his feet In a few moments, he was snoring.

Macey sat watching the keepers and polishing the flat sides of his gun with the cuff of his shirt sleeve. He felt pretty tired, too, but he'd be able to keep awake for an hour. A leader had to keep awake. And he'd got plenty to think about. All the excitement of the day—and the way he'd fixed everything.... Yes, he'd been pretty smart....

The keepers had no difficulty at all in staying awake. Apart from anything else, they were so uncomfortable with their hands tied behind them that even dozing was out of the question. From time to time one of them would make a remark in a low voice, but none of them felt like discussion while Macey could overhear them. Mostly' they sat in silence, sunk in their different thoughts. They, too, had plenty to think about.

For all of them, the situation had the qualities of a nightmare. It was horrible, it was vivid, and it was disorderly. Robeson felt the humiliation of the seizure most acutely because it was he who had been in charge. He couldn't see what he could have done to prevent it but he still felt that he'd somehow failed in responsibility.

It seemed shameful that three youths should have been able to take over the tower so easily. His only consolation was that the lighthouse was still functioning. The fog signal was sounding regularly, the glow of the revolving light still showed through the window. . . . The main thing now was to do everything possible to assist and hurry the departure of these hoodlums. Once they were back ashore, the police would soon take care of them, If Macey had killed a man, as he'd said, they were probably wanted already—no doubt that was why they had stolen the boat. . . . Robeson weighed the prospects. The cruiser could well have sustained fresh, damage—but as the sea had been so calm, there was certainly a chance it hadn't. As for the leak, if anyone could make the boat watertight again, Mitchell could. With luck, the nightmare might be over in twelve hours. In the meantime, they must avoid any rash action. Robeson had no mind to end his career as a lightkeeper with a ghastly tragedy. . . .

Mitchell's thoughts were less constructive, less restrained. The indignity of his position, roped up on the floor, was almost more than he could bear. Anger and hatred consumed him. It was intolerable that these shore rats should have invaded the tower. If only he could get his hands on one of them . . .! Just to look at Macey made the blood pound in his head. "King" Macey, indeed . . .! The vain, stupid oaf! And that creature, Hines. . . . Well, there was going to be a day of reckoning, all right. . . .

Lowe's thoughts were different again. The events of the night had deeply shocked as well as scared him. Several times in his young life he'd known alarming occasions, for danger was inseparable from the sea, but he'd never imagined anything of this sort. People like Macey and Hines were wholly outside his experience—indeed, he couldn't understand how anyone could *be* like that. He'd met such people in books, but not in life. He was appalled by the callousness of Macey, who could shoot a man dead and not show even a trace of feeling about it. He felt sickened by the sadistic beastliness of Hines. And their behaviour seemed all the worse because they had been rescued from the sea, when they might easily have been drowned, and treated kindly, and fed. . . .

How *could* anyone show such ingratitude . . .? To Lowe, the whole night had been a hideous revelation. He felt thankful that he had had the responsibility of trying to cope—he wouldn't have known what to do. Robeson was wise and cautious, a man you could have complete faith in. He'd shown that already. If he hadn't been cautious there would probably have been more bloodshed by now. Lowe hated the thought of any violence—and he was scared stiff of Macey's gun. He'd try not to show it, of course—he'd do his best to keep cool. . . . All the same, it wasn't going to be easy, even for a few hours. That dead look in Macey's eyes gave him the creeps. . . .

Macey and Hines did two guard shifts each, snatching what sleep they could get in between. Then the grey of morning, began to show at the window and Macey got up from his chair and sluiced his face at the sink. "Goin' to see what the weather's like outside," he told. Hines. He looked at the keepers, heavy-eyed after their wakeful night. "Any way o' gettin' out up top, fellers?"

Robeson told him there was a gallery.

"Okay. . . . Keep an eye on 'em, Chris."

Macey climbed to the lantern room, glanced up briefly at the revolving optic, and went out through the door. He saw with satisfaction that the fog had cleared a little. Visibility should be just about right, he thought, for their trip to the shore.

He leaned over the red-painted railing and looked down at the rocks. The tide had gone down a long way and several bits of the reef were exposed. Rust red where the weed didn't hide it, it reached out in a star of jagged fingers for as much as two hundred yards. The ridge where the cruiser had stranded was exposed all along its length. It was higher than the rock on which the tower was built, but its top was a mere razor edge. The cruiser was perched diagonally across it and leaning now at a very sharp angle. The surface of the sea wasn't quite as calm as it had been the night before, but it still looked pretty quiet.

Reassured, Macey returned to the living-room, rousing Baker and Rosie with a bang on the bedroom door as he went past.

"Weather okay?" Hines asked.

"Just the ticket, mate. We better get started on things ..." He looked at Robeson. "What about that light up there? Goin' to keep it on all day?"

"If you'll take the ropes off," Robeson said, "I'll go and put it out."

"Not so fast, feller. . . . Where's the switch?"

"In the lantern room."

"Can the kid do it?" Macey jerked his head contemptuously towards Lowe, who was sitting pale and tense between the others.

"Of course."

"Untie the kid, Chris, an' take him up. . . . Got your knife?

"You bet."

"Okay ..." Macey watched Hines undo Lowe's ropes. "If he wants to go to the gents' he can ..." He, broke off as the foghorn blasted. "Can't we save that thing off, too?"

"Have a look, Jim," Robeson said.

Lowe moved stiffly to the window. "Not yet, Rob ..."

"Go on!" Macey said. "There ain't much fog now."

"There's enough. . . ."

Anxiety showed in Robeson's face. After a moment he said, "If the foghorn's switched off too soon, Macey, someone may report it isn't working. . . . You wouldn't want that to happen, would you?"

Macey saw the point. "Well, suit yourself. . . . Take the kid up, Chris." Hines flicked his knife out and went off with Lowe.

Macey turned to Mitchell. "You all set to fix the boat, bright boy?"

"Yes," Mitchell said.

You got tools an' things?"

"Yes—down in the engine room."

Macey nodded. "We'll take a gander after breakfast."

Voices sounded outside the door and Baker and Rosie came in. Rosie was newly made up, with rouge and mascara and green eye shadow.

"Hallo, Rosie girl," Macey said. "You get some kip?"

"Not much ..." Rosie sounded peevish. "When we going to leave?"

"I told you—soon as we float."

"Can't be too soon for me, I can tell you. . . . All that row . . ." She eyed the keepers. "They been sitting there like that all night?"

"'Course."

She looked quickly away. "What's for breakfast?"

"You tell me," Macey said, "Nice cup o' char an' some eggs, I reckon. There's eggs in the cupboard."

"Who's going to get it?"

"You are, baby."

Rosie tossed her head. "What d'you think I am—cook, or something?"

"That's right," Macey said. "Tommy'll help you."

"Where the others?"

"Gone to put the light out."

"Oh, well—s'pose I'd better. . . ." Rosie teetered over to the stove. Baker was already getting things out of the cupboard.

In a few minutes Hines came back with Lowe. "Light's out," he said. "Wotcher, Tommy."

Rosie sniffed. Baker said, "Wotcher, Chris."

"Goin' to tie the kid up again?" Hines asked.

"Just his feet," Macey said. "They can all have their hands free for a bit o' grub, seein' they're behavin' all right." He stood well back with gun while Hines fiddled with the ropes.

"Eggs is ready," Baker called. "Come an' get 'em."

Rosie started to pass mugs of tea round. Hines cut hunks of bread from the loaf. Baker distributed the boiled eggs. There was a shortage of crockery and cutlery, but they managed.

"Homely, ain't it?" Hines said.

Macey looked at his watch. The time was just coming up to eight o'clock. "Let's 'ave the news, Chris."

Hines reached for the portable radio and switched it on. The announcer was just beginning to read the news headlines. The first item was about a big bomb explosion in Johannesburg. The second was about the hold-up at Salmoth. . . . Hines glanced uncertainly at Macey.

"Leave it on," Macey said, "I wanna hear it. . . . Don't matter about these geezers—they can't do nothin'. . . ."

The headlines ended. The report of the bomb explosion was largely lost in the blare of the fog signal. The noise died away just in time for the start of the item.

The announcer said: "The manager of the Majestic Cinema, at Salmoth, Devon, was shot dead last night when three youths and a girl in a stolen car made an armed raid on the cinema during thick fog. While one of the youths held up the cashier with a knife and emptied the till, another stood at the door of the cinema with a gun. When the manager, Mr. George Dixon, came out of the auditorium, the second man shot him through the head. The two gangsters then made off in the car with the third youth and the girl. Currency notes amounting to about a hundred and twenty pounds were stolen. According to Mrs. Blount, the cashier, Mr. Dixon was shot at close range, quite deliberately, as he turned to go back into the cinema."

Rosie gave Macey a startled look.

"Lyin' old bag," Macey said. "I told you, the bloke went for me. . . ."

There were descriptions now—of the car, of Macey's camel-hair coat and strong build, of Hine's clothes, of Baker's youth and Rosie's bright blonde hair. The gangsters, the report said, were believed to be still in Salmouth, and the town was being combed for them.

The item ended. Macey gestured, and Hines switched off. Baker munched thoughtfully. Hines looked at the keepers and grinned.

"There you are," Macey said, "they're searchin' for us in the town still—don't know about the boat. . . . Getaway's goin' to be easy. . . ." He was glad he'd listened. He could see from the faces of the three keepers the the report had made quite an impression on them. They'd realise now what sort of man they were dealing with. Someone who could plan a raid and get away with it. And shoot straight, too. They'd be extra careful from now on. . . . Not that they amounted to much, anyway. Macey despised them. They were a pretty dumb lot, sitting there in a row, not speaking. . . .

He drained his mug and pushed his chair back. "Right," he said, "now we gotta get the boat fixed." He motioned to Hines. "Untie bright boy's feet . . . Tommy, you better come with me an' Mitchell . . . Chris, you watch the other two. . . ."

They filed down the spiral staircase, Baker in the lead, Mitchell in the middle, Macey bringing up the rear with the gun. They stopped for a moment at the engine room so that Mitchell could collect a bag of tools and some repair materials. Then they continued to the entrance room, went down the ladders in the same order, and picked their way carefully over the narrow ridge of rock to the boat. The tide had turned, but it would be hours yet before the water reached the level of the cruiser.

Mitchell looked around at the slightly ruffled sea; up at the sky through the thinning fog. He sniffed the faint breeze. Then, without comment, he turned to the old hull. Its bottom, on the exposed side, was patched in several places. He scraped away some of the weed that covered it and found wood bare of paint and obviously soft. He had rarely seen a less seaworthy vessel—the hull looked fit only for firewood. He made his way slowly round it, followed closely by Baker and at a safer distance by Macey. At the forefoot, he stopped. The cause of the bad leak was apparent without further searching. Two planks had sprung where they joined the stem and the gap was wide enough for him to put his finger in.

"Blimey!" Baker said. So that was what they'd done when they'd hit the post!

"Reckon you can fix it?" Macey asked.

Mitchell shrugged. "I can try."

"Better make it good, bright boy. . . . You never know, I might decide to 'ave you along with us. . . ."

With a sour look, Mitchell set to work. He knew he couldn't make a proper job of it, the wood was too rotten, but he could botch something up. Enough to get them away, maybe . . . Macey stood by with the gun.

Baker turned and gazed up at the tower. It was the first time he'd seen a lighthouse close to, in daylight. It was pale grey, with a red lantern and gallery. He liked its slim, tapering shape. It looked enormously high and very strong and he wondered how anyone had ever managed to build it there. . . .

Macey said, "Might as well bail the old tub out, Tommy. . . . Start dry, any rate. . . ."

"Sure, King. . . ." Baker climbed in over the low side of the listing hull. Some of the water taken aboard had already poured out through the hole in the planks, but there was still a lot trapped inside. Baker took the bucket and bailed till he could no longer scoop anything up. Then he had a look at the fuel tank. It was hard to tell how much oil there was left with the boat at such a sharp angle, but there seemed to be plenty. Enough for eight miles, anyway. . . . He went into the saloon to take a look round there. He hadn't been able to see the boat properly in the dark and he was interested. He examined the bits of gear and poked about in the lockers. In one of them he found what looked like a bundle of yellow rubber tied up with rope. When he undid the rope and opened the bundle he discovered to his surprise that it was a small rubber dinghy. It had paddles and a hand pump for blowing it up, all secured in pockets.

He took it on to the cabin top and inflated it. It was about five feet long and slightly pear-shaped. He called to Macey and held it up to show him. "Found it inside, King. . . . Might be useful for doin' the last bit to the shore."

Macey grunted. "Don't look safe to me."

"Reckon it'd be okay for two, if we was careful."

"Well, let's hope we don't need it, mate. . . . You can come down now—bright boy's pretty well finished."

Baker left the dinghy on the cabin top and joined the others on the rocks. Mitchell had nailed a piece of sheet metal over the gap in the stem and plugged the edges with some plastic compound from a tin.

Baker fingered the repair. "Looks all right, King, don't it?"

Mitchell stood back. "It's the best I can do, anyway,"

"Okay," Macey said. "Pick up your tools an' get back into the lighthouse. . . ." Until the sea approached the boat there was nothing more they could do outside.

The foghorn blasted. Macey said, "How about turnin' that thing off now?"

Mitchell looked around, and nodded.

"Where's the switch—in the lantern?"

"Yes."

"I'll come up with you," Macey said. "Gets on your ruddy nerves, that does. . . ."

They had barely got back to the living-room when, somewhere overhead, a bell rang loudly. Macey jumped. "What the hell's that?"

"It's the telephone," Robeson said.

"For you?"

"I expect so."

"What they want?"

The keeper looked at his watch—then shrugged. "I've no idea."

Macey hesitated—but only for a moment. "You better answer it. . . . Tie Mitchell up, Chris, an' let Robeson go. . . . Quick as you can!"

There was a scramble over the ropes, in which Baker joined. In a few seconds, Mitchell was secured again and Robeson freed. Macey motioned to him to get up. "Where's the blower?"

"In the service room."

"Right—up you go. . . . If either o' these geezers makes a move, Chris, stick him . . .!" Macey prodded Robeson with the gun and followed him up the staircase.

"Now I'm warnin' you," Macey said, as they approached the telephone. "You don't know nothing see. . . . You say one word you shouldn't just one word, feller, an' I'll shove a bullet straight in your guts. So watch it . . ." He held the gun a foot away from Robeson's stomach, his finger on the trigger.

Robeson lifted the receiver. "Swirlstone Lighthouse," he said, "Principal Keeper here. . . ." His voice was firm but there was sweat on his forehead.

"Morning, Skipper . . ." The voice at the other end was loud and clear—Macey could hear the words plainly. "Sergeant Dukes here—Salmouth police."

"Morning," Robeson said.

"Did you happen to hear about the raid on the Majestic last night?"

"Yes—it was on the radio."

"Well, we think the gang got away in a boat. There's a cruiser missing from the yacht basin—thirty-footer named *Heron*. Old tore-out, dirty grey colour. . . . You haven't seen anything of it, I suppose?"

Macey's finger tightened on the gun.

"No, I haven't seen her," Robeson said. "Been too much fog about."

"That's what I thought. . . . Well, keep your eyes skinned, will you, and let us know at once if you see any sign of her."

"I will . . ."

"Thanks a lot. Bye. . . ." The telephone clicked at the other end. Robeson hung up.

Macey gave an approving nod. "You just saved a life, feller . . .!" He picked up the record book from the table and started to turn its pages. "Get many calls 'ere?"

"Not many."

Macey stopped at an entry—for the previous day. "What's this—'Report to shore, 1040 hours'?"

"One of us rings up the coastguard every morning," Robeson said.

"What for?"

"It's a routine call. Just to report everything's in order and give the weather situation."

Macey turned a page. " 'Report to shore, 1645 hours. . . .' When's that?"

"Quarter to five in the afternoon."

"You ring afternoons too, eh?"

"That's right," Robeson said. "Twice a day."

"Always the same time?"

44

"Between ten-thirty and eleven in the mornings," Robeson said, "and between four-thirty and five in the afternoons. It's left to me to decide just when."

Macey looked at his watch. His eyes narrowed. "Reckon you been holdin' out on me, feller. . . . It's 10.40 now. Wasn't you goin' to ring to-day?"

Robeson mopped his forehead with his sleeve. "It wouldn't make any difference. . . . If I didn't ring the coastguard by eleven, he'd ring me."

"Sure—an' he'd think there was somethin' wrong, wouldn't he . . .? You better get back on that blower quick!"

"I'll have to check the weather first," Robeson said.

"You do that—but step on it. . . ."

Robeson went to the window and looked out, made a note of the barometer reading and temperature and wind force, climbed to the gallery with Macey at his heels and glanced at the weather vane at the top of the lantern. When he returned to the telephone it was five to eleven. He gave the coastguard's number. "Hallo, Fred . . ."

The report took only a few moments. Macey listened carefully, but there was nothing in the brief, business-like conversation he could find to object to.

"Right," he said, as Robeson hung up again, "back you go downstairs. . . . Reckon that's fixed 'em all!"

An hour later Macey went up to the gallery by himself for another reconnaissance. What he saw didn't please him. The fog had cleared completely and a pale sun was shining. For the first time there were ships in sight—two small steamers going into Salmouth, and several more away on the horizon. To the north, the land was visible—a long, high cliff, faintly outlined against the sky. That would be Sheep Head. Eight miles. . . .

Macey frowned. He reckoned that it wouldn't take more than about an hour to reach the shore once they'd started—but now that the cruiser had been reported missing and the fog had gone it was going to be a dangerous hour. Everyone would be on the lookout for the boat—ships, coastguards, the lot. . . . The way things had turned out, maybe they ought to wait until dusk before they set off. There were houses on Sheep Head and they'd be lit up after dark, so there'd be no trouble about finding the way. They could float off at the time they'd planned and just stick around near the lighthouse for a while. That way there'd be no danger. . . . The hazards of the actual crossing hardly worried Macey at all. They'd made it to the tower, so why shouldn't they make it back again? There was a bit of cloud over in the east and more wind round the gallery, but the sea didn't look too bad. . . .

He went down presently to tell the others about his change of plan. Baker was standing at the window, looking rather thoughtful. Rosie was pencilling her eyebrows at the mirror over the sink. Hines had found some dance music on the radio and was jigging to it. . . . Macey told him to turn it off, and gave his revised situation report, "Reckon we'll wait," he said, "an' push off around half past five. . . . That's the best time. Do it easy then. . . ."

The postponement sounded sensible and no one raised any objection. But Baker brought up another matter that was on his mind.

"You thought what we goin' to do about the keepers, King, when we clear out?"

"'Course," Macey said—though he hadn't.

"Well, what?" Hines asked.

"If we untie them before we go," Baker said, "they'll get straight on the blower an' tell the cops we're on our way. . . . An' we'll be nicked for sure."

"What we gotta untie them for?" Hines said. "What's wrong with just leavin' them as they are?"

"If we leave them tied they won't be able to eat or nothin'. . . . Can't do that, Chris."

"That's right," Rosie said. "Can't do that, King. They ain't bad fellers . . ."

"We can leave them tied loose," Hines said, "so it takes them a bit o' time to get free."

Baker shook his head. "Wouldn't take them long if they was tied loose. . . . They'd be on the blower in no time."

A sudden gleam came into Hines's eyes. "Well, there's an easy way out o' that, mate. Bust the ruddy blower . . .! Wotcher say, King, shall I go an' bust it? That'll fix 'em. . . ."

"Blimey, you kids don't 'alf yap," Macey said. "Bustin' the blower ain't necessary."

"What's your idea, then?"

"Leave 'em tied up," Macey said. "They'll be okay. Robeson's supposed to ring up the coastguard by five o'clock, see. When he don't, the coastguard'll ring him, an' he won't get no answer, an' pretty soon a boat'll come out to see what's up. . . . By that time we'll be miles away, so it won't matter."

Baker looked relieved. "Cor, you're smart, King."

It was a little after one o'clock when Macey began to feel anxious about the way the weather was shaping. They'd had dinner, of sorts; they'd put a bit of food and water aboard *Heron;* they were all set to float off as soon as the sea lifted the boat. But when Macey went up to the gallery for a final look round, he had a shock. The clouds had spread over the sky and a stiff breeze was blowing. The surface of the sea was flecked with white. At the foot of the tower, waves were beginning to throw spray over the rocks.

He stood for a while, frowning at the scene. Then he went down to tell the others. "Sea ain't like what it was this morning," he said. "Don't look so good to me."

Baker and Rosie went to the window and gazed out. They could see the white horses—and hear the wind piping up, too.

"Changed quick, ain't it?" Rosie said.

Baker nodded. "Let's go down an' have a dekko, Rosie. See it better from the bottom. . . ."

They went quickly down to the entrance room. As Baker got the door open, Hines joined them. They all looked out towards the boat. The ridge of rock they'd have to walk over was still uncovered, but the sea was swirling hungrily around it. Where the waves were hitting the edge of the reef there was a lot of foam. The wind blew gustily.

"Ain't *too* bad," Baker said, after a moment. "Reckon we'll be able to make it all right, once we get clear."

Hines seemed more doubtful. "What you think, Rosie?"

She looked at the seething water below them, then out to the open sea. "It *is* better away from the rock . . ."

"Yeah, an' that's where we'll be," Baker said. "All we gotta do is float off—then we'll be okay."

A wave slopped over the ridge in a smother of white. Hines said, "Well, I can tell you this, mate—if we goin' to get in that boat we gotta do it ruddy quick."

"That's right," Baker said, "Next five minutes, I reckon."

"I'll go an' tell King." Hines darted away up the tower. . . .

Macey was standing by the window. "What's it look like down there, Chris?"

"Ruddy awful," Hines said. "Might jus' make it, though, if we go now."

Macey picked up his coat, made sure that the keepers' ropes were tight, and followed Hines down. At the entrance door he stood in silence, gazing out at the rising sea.

"What we going to do, King?" Rosie said. "Ain't we going?"

"I dunno. . . ."

"Well, we got to make up our minds. It ain't no good just looking."

"I reckon it's okay," Baker said. "I reckon we oughter just climb in an' wait in the boat."

Macey grunted. "It's me what says, Tommy."

"Sure, King . . ."

"Don't look so good to me."

"Nor to me," Hines said.

"May be better to-morrow . . ."

A wave hit the weather side of the reef with a crash and spray flew up almost to the set-off. The wind seemed to be getting stronger every moment.

"Reckon we'd be nutters to try it now," Macey said. "Look at that . . .!"

A big wave had broken over the whole ridge, roaring along it from end to end and covering it with creaming foam.

Rosie stared down at it. That was where they'd have to cross. "I don't reckon it's safe, either," she said. "Not now . . ."

They stayed and watched. There was no longer any question of getting to the boat, but the spectacle was fascinating. As the sea rose, the whole area of the reef became one vast cauldron of boiling foam. The waves were beginning to crash against the inert side of the cruiser's hull and break over it in fountains of spray. Baker thought wryly of his hard bailing that morning. Water kept pouring into the cockpit. . . . They were all thankful now that they hadn't attempted to cross the ridge. It would have been awful out there in the boat, waiting. It looked really frightening. . . .

Worse was to come—much worse. Presently, the hull stirred. On a wave, it rose a little, and fell back. Up at the entrance door, high above the water, they heard the crack as it dropped. Another wave lifted it—and another. For long moments it was lost to sight in the heavy spray. A sea washed over it, carrying away the rubber dinghy that Baker had left on the roof. A huge one came, and the boat rose like a lift and fell like a stone. Now it was pounding hard all the time, rising and falling and slamming down with fearful violence on the jagged spine of the rock. Sounds of rending wood reached the watchers above the noise of the waves. Planks were beginning to come away from the stem. Planks were falling out of the sides.
. . .

Then, before their awed eyes, the cruiser broke up. The whole cabin top came adrift and floated away. The bows and the stern took up a crazy angle to each other. Battered by the sea and the rock, hammered and holed by its own heavy engine, the stricken hull hardly looked like a boat any more. Another big wave caught it broadside on—and it plunged off the rock into deep water and sank. There was nothing left to look at but a few floating planks.
. . .

Chapter Three

In a slow file, they climbed back up the tower. The disaster had struck so unexpectedly and with such shattering finality that for the moment they were left speechless. The sight of the sea's power had been a subduing experience for all of them—the picture of the disintegrating wreck would stay in their minds for many a day. . . . Even more subduing was the thought of the consequences. They were far from seeing all the implications yet, but one thing was plain enough—they no longer had any means of escaping from the lighthouse.

Dejectedly, they trooped into the living-room. The keepers were stili firmly tied. Robeson said, "Well—what's happened?" He looked at Macey.

Macey, his mind busy with their predicament, seemed not to hear.

"Boat's smashed up," Baker said. "Just fell to bits."

Robeson nodded, gravely. It was the unwanted outcome that, since dinner-time, the keepers had fore-seen. They knew how quickly the sea could get up and the effect it would have over the reef. The rising wind, combined with Mitchell's description of the rotten hull, had left little doubt in their minds. . . . Now, like the gangsters, they had a new situation to face.

Robeson made an effort to reassert his authority while the four were still suffering from shock. "Well," he said, as though there were now no room for argument, "that seems to be it, doesn't it? You may as well untie us and give up."

"Think so?" Macey said.

"There's nothing else you can do. . . . I'll get on the RT, and as soon as this bit of a blow is over a boat will come out and take you off."

"You're nuts," Macey said.

"It's common sense, boy. . . . You're stuck here now—you can't get away. And you'll be taken off in any case when the next relief boat comes out."

Mitchell joined in, "It'll only be the worse for you all in the end, if you go on giving trouble."

"He's right," Robeson said. He was looking particularly at Baker and Rosie. "If you give up now it'll count in your favour. It's the best thing you can do for yourselves. . . . Get these ropes off us, and hand over your gun and knife, and I'll promise you all decent treatment until you're taken off."

"You ain't in no position to make promises," Macey said.

"That's my offer, anyway. . . . For heaven's sake, boy, keeping us like this till the relief comes isn't going to help you—you'll have to face the music in the end. . . . It just means we'll all be very uncomfortable."

Hines said, "When's the relief comin', Daddy-O?"

Robeson glanced at the calendar on the wall. "It's not due till March 12th. May be longer if the weather turns bad."

Macey gave a grant of satisfaction. "Ain't no hurry, then, is there? That's nearly a month. . . ."

"A month or six weeks, it'll be the same in the end."

"How d'you know . . .? Plenty o' time for something to turn up in a month. Plenty o' time to think o' something. . . . Any rate, we ain't givin' up."

"But surely, Macey, you must see . . ."

Macey cut him short. "You're wastin' your breath, feller. Things is goin' to stay just the way they are—an' no argument." He moved towards the door. "Look after 'em for a bit, Chris."

"Where you off to, King?"

"Seein' as how we may be here for quite a while," Macey said, "I reckon I'll take a gander round the place. . . . Ain't properly been over it yet."

He started his purposeful scrutiny at the bottom of the tower. First, the entrance room, where he'd noticed a couple of round manhole covers in the floor. He prised one of them open, and peered down. There was a tank underneath—a large one. He unscrewed a cap and saw that the tank was nearly full of fresh water. It was about ten feet across and obviously held many hundreds of gallons, perhaps thousands. They weren't going to die of thirst, anyway. . . .

He replaced the cover, stopped for a moment to examine the entrance doors and their fastenings, and went on to the engine room, which he hadn't seen before. There were three small, neat generators, bright with green paint and burnished brass. Close by was a tall, rectangular control panel with a variety of buttons and switches. In cupboards around the walls there were tools and oil cans and spare parts. The air smelt of diesel fuel, but the room itself was spotlessly clean. Macey found a short iron bar in one of the tool boxes, and took it away with him.

He looked briefly into the battery and oil room above and then continued up to the store room, where he poked around for quite a while. There were stores there of almost every description—coils of rope in many sizes, stacked cans of paint, more cans of turpentine and paraffin, brushes and brooms and cleaning materials, hurricane lamps, spare crockery and utensils, and several large boxes of tinned food. In the cupboards Macey found more food, of the sort that wouldn't go bad—sugar and jam and tea and coffee and dry biscuits. . . . They obviously weren't going to die of starvation, either.

He went on up to the winch room and casually tried the handle. Like everything else in the tower the machinery was well cared for, and the handle went round with scarcely a sound. He opened up some more cupboards and found solid fuel and wood for the stove.

He skipped the living-room, where the others were, but made a thorough inspection of the bedroom. There were three lower bunks curving round the wall of the room and two upper ones without bedclothes that looked as though they weren't used much. All the berths had curtains, and strip lighting above the pillows. Macey pulled out the lockers underneath and turned over the clothes and possessions of the keepers. He wanted to know everything about the place. . . .

The service room didn't detain him long. The only thing he hadn't noticed there before was a range of three small refrigerators, inset into the wall. One for each of the keepers. He examined their contents. They were all full of perishable foods. Yes, there'd be plenty to eat. . . . His glance fell on the RT set and he suddenly remembered about the regular calls that Robeson had to make. Good job he'd thought of that! Good job, too, that he hadn't let Chris smash the set, or a boat would have been out in no time. He looked at his watch. Another half-hour to go—but he mustn't forget. . . .

He climbed to the lantern room and mounted the short ladder to the optic platform. It was the first time he'd had a good look at the light. He finished his tour out on the gallery, noting the flagpole, the lightning-conductor, the wind vane at the top, and the short step-ladder for washing the upper part of the lantern. . . .

The lighthouse was quite a place, he thought, as he went down to join the others. Quite a place . . .!

There was still an air of dejection in the living-room. Rosie was gazing out of the window in a forlorn way. Baker was sitting with his head bowed and his fists against his cheeks. Hines was stretched out in another chair, idly flicking his knife in and out.

He looked up as Macey came in, "Well—you 'ad a good dekko?"

Macey nodded. "Nice bit o' property . . ."

Hines eyed the iron bar. "What's that you got, King?"

"Cosh for Tommy." Macey tapped Baker on the shoulder and gave him the bar. "Never know—might come in useful. . . . These geezers been behavin' all right?"

"No," Hines said, "they been bellyachin'."

Robeson stirred. "There are' all sorts of jobs to be done, Macey. Who's going to do them?"

"What jobs?"

"You don't suppose the tower runs itself. There's a routine that has to be kept to . . ."

"All I seen any o' you do," Macey said, "is pull a few switches. Reckon we can do that, eh, Chris?"

"Reckon so, King."

"Such as what?"

"The optic has to be polished every day, for a start. It should have been done this morning. . . . All the lantern panes have to be washed, too—inside and out. Fifty-six of them. If these jobs aren't done, the light won't be as strong and clear as it should be."

Macey grunted. "Anything else?"

"That's just the beginning. . . . The generator has to be serviced. The batteries have to be checked. The tower has to be cleaned every day. The rooms have to been done out in turn. A hundred steps have to be swept. Water has to be pumped to the tank here. Coal has to be fetched. All the brass has to be polished. . . ."

Macey gave a gracious nod. "Well, that's okay with me. . . . Don't want the place to get in a muck, do we, Rosie?"

Rosie looked as though she wasn't passionately interested either way.

Macey considered. "Tell you what I'll do," he said after a moment. "One o' you geezers can go free at a time, see. Take it in turns, like. Bloke what's free can do the chores."

Robeson's face cleared a little.

"He'll be watched, mind you. He'll have a guard on him, every second. An' 'e hadn't better start no funny business, or I'll see him off meself. . . . That clear?"

"You've got the gun," Mitchell said. "That's clear enough."

"Okay, bright boy—don't you forget it. . . ." Macey looked at his watch. "Time for you to get on the blower now," be said to Robeson, "Let 'im go, Chris. . . ."

As Robeson reached for the receiver, Macey checked him. "Before you starts feller, I got another word o' warnin' for you."

"Well?"

"It's like this, see. You'll be doin' a lot o' talkin' on this thing, as time goes on. . . . I'll be here listening, o' course—but maybe you think you can slip something through, what I wouldn't

54

understand. Somethin' you ain't never said before, what'd start Fred sussin'. . . . An' may be you could, too . . ."

Robeson waited.

"Well, in case you got anything like that in your nut, I'll tell you straight—if that relief boat comes out 'ere before March 12th I'll know it's because o' something you said on the blower, an' none o' you three geezers won't live to set eyes on it. I'll finish the lot o' you, see. It's like what I said—I ain't got nothin' to lose. . . . Okay, now you can call up your pal. . . ."

When they got back to the living-room Macey handed Robeson over to Hines. "Take him off an' put him to work, Chris, like 'e wants . . . Shouldn't think he'll give no trouble—but keep your knife out."

"Ain't we goin' to eat?" Hines said. "We didn't have no proper dinner, man."

Macey waved him away, "Rosie'll fix something. . . . I'll give you a shout when it's ready."

Hines went off with Robeson, muttering.

Rosie said, "Wish there was one big room instead of all these little ones . . . I feel kind of shut in."

Baker grinned. "Reckon we're all shut in, Rosie."

"I don't mean that, stupid. . . . It's so hot everywhere—I can't hardly breathe."

"It's cosy," Macey said. "Stop knockin' the place, will you . . .?"

"Well, why's it so hot when it's winter?"

I dunno. . . . 'Spect it's the engine goin' so much. Want me to open the window?"

"No, it don't matter . . ." Rosie undid the top button of her sweater. "What we going to eat?"

"Up to you, Rosie girl. . . . There's meat in them fridges upstairs."

"I ain't cookin' no meat," Rosie said. "Wouldn't know how. . . . Ain't there no tins?"

"In the cupboard," Mitchell told her. "Over there."

Rosie crossed to the cupboard and started to poke around inside. Presently she pulled out a jar. "What's this?"

"That's meat," Lowe said. "I cooked it yesterday."

Rosie looked at it distastefully. "What's all this fat on top for?"

"To keep it from going bad. It lasts nearly a month that way."

"M'm—you can have it!"

"It's very good," Lowe said. "It goes down well when all the fresh meat's gone...." He watched her fumbling with the tins. "Would you like me to do the cooking?"

"You shut your trap, kid," Macey said. "Tryin' to win a medal or somethin' ...?"

"Why shouldn't he do the cooking?" Rosie said.

"Because I say not."

Rosie pouted. "Well, don't blame me, that's all ..." She chose a couple of tins. "Stewed steak—how's that?"

"Sounds all right for a start."

"We going to feed all this lot?"

"'Course," Macey said. "Gotta keep their strength up, seein' they're so keen on workin'."

"Here you are, then—peas and carrots, too."

Baker found some saucepans, and a tin-opener, and opened the tins. Rosie tipped out the contents and put the saucepans on the stove. Macey sat back like a sultan.

"Bread ain't up to much," Rosie said. "Ain't there any fresh?" She looked at Lowe.

Lowe shook his head. "We couldn't bake to-day."

"Mean you make your own bread?"

"Of course—we have to. Every day."

"Do you do the baking?"

"We all bake our own."

Rosie stared. "What—just for yourselves!"

"It's a custom of the service."

"Reckon they're scared o' bein' poisoned," Macey said. "Don't trust each other ..."

"We order our own food supplies, too," Lowe told Rosie. "The relief brings them out with him, different for everybody.... And whoever's cook for the day cooks what each man says. We hardly ever eat the same as each other."

"Well, you're going to now," Rosie saids smiling. "Stewed steak and peas and carrots.... It's about ready, too."

Macey went to the door and called, "Chris ...!"

Hines came in behind Robeson, his flick-knife open. Robeson went to the sink to wash his hands.

"Cor, them flippin' stairs!" Hines said. "Reckon they oughter have a lift in this place.... My legs don't half ache."

"Do you good, mate," Macey told him. "Bit of exercise."

Mitchell said, "What did you do, Rob?"

"Cleaned the optic. Greased the generator ..."

"What's the weather like now?"

"Settling down. Looks as though it's going to be quiet again. ..."

Hines was still grumbling. "Three times we went up an' down them ruddy stairs.... Doin' this an' fetchin' that. These, geezers is like ruddy chars ..." He looked into the saucepans. "Blimey, is that what we goin' to eat?"

"If it don't suit you," Rosie said, "you know what you can do. ..." She began to serve the food out.

Macey said, "Better tie Robeson up again.... Just his feet, Chris."

"What, me? Why can't Tommy do it?"

"He's helpin' Rosie.... Come on, mate."

With a scowl, Hines secured Robeson beside the other two. Then Baker passed the food round and they all fell on it hungrily. Hines had taken the only available chair, so Baker had to eat standing. No one talked much....

Directly the meal was over Macey began to give his instructions again, allocating jobs, "You make a cup o' char, Tommy.... The kid can do the washin' up.... Let 'im go, Chris."

There was more untying. Lowe got to work on the dishes with quiet efficiency. He was used to being the dogsbody, Macey thought.

Robeson was eyeing the window. Presently he said, "It's about time the light went on."

Macey reviewed his forces. "Okay—you better finish the plates, Rosie. Tommy, you go with the kid.... Take your cosh with you."

"I ain't afraid of him, King," Baker said.

"'Course you ain't. . . . 'E looks big but it's just puppy fat."

Baker and Lowe departed. In a few minutes the generator started to hum. Then the light came on. Robeson could see it from where he sat. There was a mirror fastened at an angle outside the living-room window, a useful fitting that Mitchell had put up, which served as a tell-tale. Robeson lit his pipe. That was one worry off his mind, at any rate.

Lowe came in, with Baker behind him. Macey said, "Okay—tie the kid up again, Chris."

Hines groaned. "'Struth, King, how long we goin' on with this lark?"

"Till I say not."

"I'll do it if you like, King," Baker said.

"You wait till you're given the nod, Tommy. . . . We goin' to have discipline in this place, see?"

Hines did the tying.

"Well—now what we goin' to do . . .?" Hines looked at his watch. "Six o'clock, King—time for the news. Want it?"

"'Course," Macey said. "Gotta keep track o' what's happenin'. . . ."

Hines reached for the radio and switched it on.

The Salmouth affair held second place in the list of items. The announcer said, "The three youths and the girl concerned in the hold-up at the Salmouth cinema, where the manager, Mr. Dixon, was shot dead, are now believed to have left Salmouth Harbour in a stolen boat, a thirty-foot grey motor crusier named *Heron*. Police and coastguard launches have been searching along the coast all day, but so far no trace of the cruiser has been found. The French police have been alerted, in case the gang should attempt to cross the Channel, and all shipping has been asked to keep a sharp lookout . . ."

Hines turned the volume down. "Lookin' out ain't goin' to do 'em much good," he said with a grin. "How d'you like that, eh?—tellin' the French rozzers?"

"Just what we want," Macey said. "Means no one won't come snoopin' round here. . . . Man, we sure started something."

Hines cackled. "How's your parley-voo, Tommy?"

Baker said nothing. Neither did Rosie, In all the excitement of the day, the shooting of the manager had taken a back place in their minds. Now they'd been unpleasantly reminded of it.

Hines fiddled with the set. "How come you ain't got on telly here, Daddy-O?"

"We have," Robeson said.

"Where is it, then?"

"In a box downstairs. There's a valve gone."

"Cor, couldn't you get it fixed?"

"It went the night the relief boat left. Now we'll have to wait till next time."

"Well, if that ain't lousy luck," Hines said. "Just when we got a use for it. . . ." He continued to twiddle the radio knob, till he found some swing. "That's more like it . . ." He stood by the set, grimacing, the toe of his right foot beating time against a chair, his fingers clicking at the end of his bony wrists.

The sound drowned all talk, arrested all thought. Robeson, sitting close to the set, saw that the radio wasn't going to be a boon in the tower any longer. The keepers had always used it with discretion, in a spirit of give and take. . . . Now it seemed to take possession of the tiny space.

In the end, even Macey got tired of the noise. "Turn it off, Chris—there ain't room for that row in 'ere."

Sulkily, Hines obeyed.

They all sat in silence for a while. Then Rosie got up. "I'm tired," she said. "I'm going to bed."

"Ain't bedtime yet," Hines said.

"What of it? Nothing to stay up for, is there . . .?" Rosie stood for a moment, shaking out her hair, examining her face in the mirror. Then she went up to the bedroom.

Macey said, "We better fix up how we goin' to guard these geezers all night."

Hines groaned again. "Blimey, King, ain't we goin' to get no proper kip?"

"We gotta keep watch," Macey said, "case they get them knots untied.... We better do two hours each, see, an' Tommy can start. Then you, Chris. Bloke what comes off wakes the next one.... Okay, Tommy?"

"Sure, King."

Hines yawned. "Well, if you say so...." He gazed around the room in a jaundiced way. "This ain't 'alf a hole, ain't it ...? Like bein' in the ruddy nick."

"You ain't never been in the nick," Macey said, "so you don't know ... I can tell you, this is a ruddy palace. Some blokes don't know when they're well off."

Hines was muttering again. "Up an' down the bloody stairs.... Tie 'em up an' let 'em loose.... Follow 'em around.... What we goin' to do, King? You thought of anything yet?"

Macey frowned. "Give me time, man—we only been here a few hours."

"That's right," Baker said, "he ain't had a chance yet."

"If you're so flippin' keen to leave, mate," Macey said, "you can ruddy well swim for it.... It ain't far—only eight miles."

There were no crises during the night—but it was far from being a quiet one. The frequent changes of watch were disturbing. Mitchell was restless and complained of cramp until Baker, at the first switch-over, fetched pillows from the bedroom for all the keepers to sit on. Robeson had to go and relieve himself during Macey's first watch, which meant waking Hines to untie him and take him down the tower. One way and another, Macey felt thankful when, towards the end of his second watch, daylight showed at the window.

He washed at the sink and shaved carefully with Mitchell's razor and put on a clean shirt of Lowe's which just fitted him. A scruffy chin and a dirty collar, he decided, didn't go with his position. Robeson was sent off under Baker's escort to switch off the light and the generator, and when they returned Macey climbed to the gallery. He was feeling a bit jaded after the broken night, but the air refreshed him. It was mild for February and pleasant to stand around in. Robeson's view of the weather prospects had obviously been right. The wind had dropped again and the pewter sea was almost as calm as when they'd arrived.

Macey gazed around him with something very like contentment. It wasn't too bad, he thought, being in control of a lighthouse. In fact, he was beginning to get quite a kick out of it. It gave him a real king-of-the-castle feeling, standing here on the gallery and looking down at the shapely tower, which was all his. Knowing, too, that there were folk down below who'd do whatever he said. Not just his own gang, but the prisoners as well. He'd only got to open his mouth and they'd jump to it. He could make them do anything with his gun. They were his slaves. Six people he'd got at his beck and call—and no one to raise a voice against him, no one to interfere with him.... Things could certainly have been much worse....

He found no corresponding contentment among the others when he returned to the living-room. Rosie was moodily setting about the task of preparing breakfast for seven. Hines, with the night's stubble on his chin, was moodily cleaning his fingernails with the point of his flick-knife. Baker was gazing moodily out of the window. Robeson's head was sunk on his chest. Mitchell wore his usual expression of smouldering anger. Lowe's face was blank. A fine lot, Macey thought. A fine, lively lot on a nice morning ...!

He tried to rally them. "Sleep okay, Rosie?" he asked brightly.

"What, with you three banging about all night ...? Don't make me laugh."

"Well, you started early enough."

"Good job too ..." Rosie began to rake out the fire, noisily.

"Reckon we'll all go bonkers if we 'ave to stay here long," Hines said. "What we goin' to do, King?"

Macey gave a faint shrug. "Oh—we'll do somethin' ..."

"It's all right for you," Rosie said, "wearing other people's shirts and things.... What am I supposed to do, I'd like to know. All I got is what's in me bag. No clean clothes, no hair-brush, no proper make-up . . ."

"Go on, Rosie, you look fine."

"Well, I don't feel fine. It ain't right . . ." Rosie's tone became a little less sharp. "Ain't you got no ideas, King?"

"Course I 'ave."

"Well, tell us, King," Baker said.

"Come on, King," Hines said, "put us out of our flippin' misery."

"Ain't no problem at all," Macey said airily. "All we gotta do is wait for a small boat to come in close. . . . Like a yacht or a fishin' boat or one o' them little things, see. . . . Then we wave to 'em, like we was in trouble, an' they come in an' land to see what's up, an' we take over the boat with the gun. . . . Easy!"

Baker grinned. "That's a smashin' idea, King."

Mitchell, from the floor, gave a derisive snort.

Macey turned on him. "Well, what's wrong with it, bright boy?"

"For a start," Mitchell said, "you won't see any yachts round here in February because they're all laid up. Nor any fishing boats—they give the reef a wide berth in winter. . . . In any case, they wouldn't be able to land."

"Why wouldn't they?" Macey didn't care much either way, but he felt he had to defend his plan.

"Because the weather wouldn't let them," Mitchell said.

"Looks okay to me. . . . Sea's like a ruddy pond."

Robeson joined in. "You don't suppose this is going to last, do you? In a day or two it'll be blowing again."

Macey shrugged. "What's a bit o' wind?"

"You don't understand, boy. We'll be getting gales—and they may go on for weeks. . . . Bad gales. When it really blows here, it's like the wrath of God."

Lowe, beside him, gave a nod. He remembered gales like that.

"Yeah?" Macey said. "Well, if it's all that bad, how do the blokes in the relief boat manage to land?"

"They don't," Robeson said. "Not once in twenty times. . . . It's hardly ever fit to come alongside the rock."

"How do you geezers get off, then?"

"The way you'll be taken off," Robeson said grimly.

"What way's that?"

"I'll tell you. . . . First, a big tender comes and anchors a quarter of a mile away. She lowers one of her small motor boats, with the relief and supplies. The motor boat comes in as near as it can safely get. Then it lets go its stern anchor and we throw a couple of lines and make its bows fast to the set-off, so that it's moored. . . . All the time, it's going up and down like a cork."

"Then what . . .?"

"Then another rope is thrown to the boat, and made fast, and the relief is winched up to the set-off in a breeches buoy—that's a thing you put your legs through and sit in. The man who's going off duty goes down the same way. Over the top of the waves and the rocks—and if he's lucky he finishes up in the boat. It's tough and it's dangerous—and we're always very thankful when it's done without accident."

There was a little silence.

"A bit different to what you thoughts eh?" Robeson said.

Macey shrugged again. "You can't scare me, feller—I done tougher things than that. . . . Any rate, the weather ain't like that now, so we better start lookin' for a little boat we can nobble right away."

"But Mitchell just said there wouldn't be any," Rosie said.

"'Course he did—he don't want us to try it, see? These geezers'd say anything to stop us gettin' away. . . . Something'll come along, don't you worry."

There was another short silence. Then Rosie said, "What if it don't, King?"

"What if we're still 'ere when the relief boat comes?" Baker said.

"That's right," Hines said. "You got any ideas about that, King?"

"Things ain't goin' to get that far," Macey said.

"S'pose they do. . . . You got any ideas?"

"'Course," Macey said.

"Reckon we'd just 'ave to take over the relief boat then," Baker said with a grin.

"Yeah, I can see that happenin'," Hines said.

"Don't see why not, Chris."

"Cor, they'd nab us soon as we got down there."

"Not if we was smart," Baker said. "King would 'ave to put on one o' these geezers' uniforms, see. Make out he was the keeper what was goin' to be relieved. . . . Then he'd go down on the rope an' take over the boat with the gun before they got wise to 'im, an' after that we'd all go down. . . . That breeches-buoy thing don't sound too bad to me."

Mitchell said, "You're out of your minds—all of you."

Macey pointed the gun at him as though it were a sceptre. "You keep your gate shut, bright boy."

Hines said, "What about throwin' the ropes an' all that . . .? We wouldn't know 'ow, Tommy."

"No trouble there," Baker said. "We'd 'ave to make one o' these geezers do it—same as they always do. They wouldn't dare not, if one o' them was still up in the tower with King's gun stuck into 'im."

"That's true . . ." Hines looked at Baker with new respect. "Well, it ain't a bad idea, Tommy. . . . Specially the uniform bit. . . ." He leaned back and jerked one of the keeper's blue jackets from its hook on the wall. It was Mitchell's. "Here, try it on, King . . ." He threw it across to Macey.

"Mind what you're doing," Rosie said. "Nearly went in the frying-pan, that did. . . ."

Macey held up the coat, pretending some interest. "Ain't big enough, Chris."

"Try the kid's, then . . ." Hines passed Lowe's jacket over instead. Macey put it on. It was a perfect fit.

Hines giggled. "Cripes, you look like a ruddy screw!"

"Screw's uniform ain't so smart," Macey said. He stood in front of the mirror, fingering the brass buttons, studying the effect. Baker passed him Lowe's flat peaked cap, with its Trinity House badge on the front, and Macey tried that on too.

"Looks pretty good," Baker said. "Specially the coat. . . . Why don't you keep it on, King?"

"Maybe I will," Macey said. "Suits me, don't it?"

It was Rosie who brought their wandering attention back to the matter under discussion. "S'pose you did take over the motor boat," she said. "What would you do with the blokes what was in it?"

"Take 'em with us," Baker said.

"But if they landed with us, they'd give us away."

"That's okay, Rosie, we'd drop 'em somewhere. Some quiet bit o' beach with a cliff where they couldn't get away easy. Then we'd find a good place to land ourselves, an' leave the boat, an' scarper. . . ."

Rosie considered the plan for a moment. Then she said, "Wouldn't the blokes in the big boat see what was happening and come after us? Or send a message to Salmouth or something?"

Baker's face fell. "I hadn't thought o' that. . . ."

"'Course they would," Hines said disgustedly. "That ain't no use, Tommy—they'd have the cops all lined up to 'elp us ashore. . . . Reckon we can forget it. . . ."

"Maybe we can work something else out, Chris."

"Any rate," Macey said, "we ain't got to decide this minute—we got plenty o' time. . . . An' I still say some little boat'll come close in before long. Soon as we've 'ad breakfast we'll start lookin' out. . . ."

With no alternative plan in sight, the small-boat watch was set up with every, outward sign of keenness. To Macey it seemed an ideal way of keeping his lieutenants occupied and contented, and he organised it with as much care as though he really thought it would achieve results. Baker and Rosie were assigned to do hourly shifts in the lantern room, with instructions to call Macey at once if any small vessel came within waving distance. At Macey's suggestion, a large white towel was taken up to the lantern and kept there with Robeson's loud hailer, ready for use. Baker took the first watch, pacing round the gallery with Robeson's binoculars on his chest and feeling as proud as a ship's officer on the bridge. Even Rosie, when she took over, kept her eyes conscientiously on the sea. But neither of them saw anything that morning except distant wisps of smoke.

Down in the living-room, Macey and Hines were going through

the irksome drill of freeing the keepers by turns so that all could have exercise and the chores could be done. Mitchell was given the first hour, and Hines accompanied him round the tower. Then Robeson was released and Macey accompanied him, supervising the regular telephone call to the shore at eleven.

It was when Hines was starting to free Lowe that he suddenly said, " King, do we really have to carry on with this tyin' lark?"

"'Course we do," Macey said.

"Don't see why—not in the daytime."

"Man, if they're all runnin' around free they'll just wait for a good chance an' then jump us."

"Not if yon got one o' them covered all the time, King. Just one o' them, it don't matter which. Sort o' hostage, see. . . . None o' them ain't goin' to start a bundle if he knows his mate's goin' to get shot for it."

Macey looked doubtful. "I dunno, Chris. . . . Might work okay—but we'd 'ave to keep watch on the old blower all the time. Else one o' them might nip in and make a call on the sly."

"Don't reckon they'd dare, King. . . . Not after what you said about shootin' the lot if a boat come out too soon."

"We'd 'ave to watch it, all the same. . . . Don't want to put temptation in their way."

"Well, it'd still be worth it, mate. . . . Be a ruddy sight easier keepin' an eye on the blower than messin' with these perishin' ropes all the time."

Macey gave a grudging nod. He didn't like accepting suggestions, particularly from Hines, but he could see this was a good one. It would save them an immense amount of trouble—and it would mean freedom to move around for practically everyone. The keepers would be able to get back to a proper routine, the tower would be more comfortable to live in, Lowe could do a bit of decent cooking. . . .

Macey looked at Robeson. As usual, the talk had flowed round the keepers as though they weren't there. "What you three geezers got to say about it?"

"I still say you'd do much better to give up," Robeson said.

"Not a chance, feller."

"Well—freeing us would be better than nothing. We could get some order back into the place—the tower's in a shocking state."

"It's the first sensible suggestion anyone's made," Mitchell said.

"Okay . . ." Macey eyed them in turn, pointing the gun at each. "Watch it, though. . . . There'll always be one o' you in front o' this, don't forget. Every flippin' second. An' at the first sound o' trouble it'll go off. . . . Right, let 'em loose, Chris."

Robeson climbed slowly to the lantern room. The strain of the ordeal was beginning to tell on him physically. His body ached from the unaccustomed sitting in a cramped position. His wrists and ankles were sore from the ropes. He felt generally out of sorts. All the same, he was relieved at the latest turn of events. He wouldn't have to worry so much about me light now. Getting back into the routine would help to speed the hours. And, after the close confinement, it felt good to be able to move around without an escort.

On his way up, he stopped at the service room to look at the barometer. It was high and steady. Hines was there, guarding the RT set and listening to pop records on the portable radio. Robeson went on up without speaking to him.

Mitchell was in the lantern room, washing the inside of the diamond windows. Out on the gallery, Baker was hopefully sweeping the horizon with the binoculars.

"Hallo, Mitch. . . ." It was the first time Robeson had been alone with his chief assistant since the seizure of the tower. "Well, we've got a chance to talk at last. . . ."

Mitchell nodded. "Do you know where Macey is?"

"He's gone down to the engine room with Jim."

"Good. . . ." Mitchell glanced through the window at Baker, and dropped his voice. "Rob, we've got to get that gun."

Robeson took out his pipe and began to fill it. "Easier said than done."

"I know—but we've got to . . ."

"Do you see any way? Macey'll shoot at the first sign of trouble—I'm sure of that."

"He can't be on the ball the whole time," Mitchell said.

"He looks pretty alert to me. I think he's got us by the short ones, Mitch. . . ."

"He has at the moment—but he could easily get careless. . . . Then we'll have our chance."

Robeson grunted. "Well, I'm all for taking a good chance, of course—but I don't want you or Jim running any stupid risks. Getting someone shot for nothing isn't going to do any good."

"We can't just let things go on . . ."

"As long as the light's all right," Robeson said, "we're doing our job—and that's what really matters. The way things are, I don't see we've anything to lose by waiting. I think we've got to keep cool heads and play along with them for a bit."

"And let them go on pushing us around!"

"I don't like it any more than you do, Mitch, but it's better than a bullet in the guts. And it won't last for ever . . ."

"It'll last a month. More if the tender's held up."

"It may not. . . . They're under a pretty big strain too, don't forget, with a murder on their hands—and it'll be worse for them when they find they can't get away. They may crack . . ."

"I doubt it," Mitchell said. "They're too dumb—they can't think more than a couple of minutes ahead. If you can call it thinking. . . . All that stuff about taking over the relief boat—did you ever hear such cock in your life . . .! Anyway, they're not worried, they don't care. . . . What a bunch!"

Robeson puffed in silence.

"Shoved around by a gang of young thugs . . .! Mitchell's lean face darkened. "A murderer, a bloody jackal, a tart and a stupid kid . . .! Christ, it's bad enough having to see their type around when you're ashore—out here it's more than I can stomach . . . I tell you, Rob, I loathe their guts. That fellow Hines makes me want to spew."

Robeson nodded. "He's the nastiest bit of work I ever saw."

"They're all rotten—dead rotten . . . I don't know what's happened to this generation, Rob. They're a lousy lot."

"I doubt if they're any worse than our lot. Mitch. . . . Not on the whole."

"What—with all this rowdyism and knife stuff and coshing people in the streets and smashing things up just for the fun of it . . .? Where's the good in them?"

"You've got to be fair," Robeson said. "They're not all like that."

"A lot of them are. More than there used to be."

Robeson shook his head. "If you ask me, Mitch, there's about the same mixture of good and bad in every generation. We old 'uns have short memories, that's the trouble. And when we start coming the heavy over all the youngsters because some of them are bad, we just show we're old. I don't reckon that's the right answer."

"What do you think's the answer, then?"

"Let them sort things out for themselves—the way we did. . . . As I see it, the fight isn't between the old and the young—it's between the young and the young, and it has to be fought out again with every new batch. Right against wrong—simple as that. A decent way of going on, against—well, whatever Macey and Hines are. . . . There's plenty of good young 'uns to-day, Mitch—and they'll come out on top all right."

Mitchell shrugged. "Wish we had a few of them here, that's all . . . with machine guns!"

Robeson gave a tired smile. "Well, remember what I said, Mitch—take it easy. . . ." He turned and climbed the short ladder to the optic platform and began to clean the light.

In a little while Rosie arrived to take over the boat watch again. She went out on to the gallery to get the binoculars from Baker and came back in with him. She'd found she could keep a lookout just as well through the windows of the lantern, and it was much warmer inside.

"Any sign of your ghost yacht yet?" Mitchell said to Baker.

Baker met his ironical gaze stolidly. "Something'll come—there's plenty o' time. . . ." He stood for a moment, watching Robeson at work on the prisms. "What you got in that bottle?" he called up.

Robeson looked down over the rail. "Cleaning spirit."

"Why don't you use water?"

"The prisms are fixed in cement," Robeson said. "Water might loosen it."

"Yeah, I see . . ." Baker still hung about. "You been up there, Rosie?"

"No. . . ."

"Let's 'ave a butcher's, then. . . ." He climbed the ladder to the circular platform. Rosie followed him. There wasn't much room, but Robeson didn't complain.

"What they for, these things?" Baker asked, running a finger down one of the triangular glass bars.

"Keep your hands off, son," Robeson said. "It's no good me polishing if you're going to make greasy fingermarks."

"Sorry," Baker said. "What they for, anyway?"

Robeson stopped polishing. "Do you really want to know?"

"Sure."

"Well, they collect up the light from the electric bulb and magnify it thousands of times and concentrate it so that it goes out in beams instead of spreading all over the place . . ." Robeson made a squeezing gesture with his hands. "Wonderful bit of work, they are—real precision job."

"Pretty, ain't they?" Rosie said. "Don't half shine."

"It's a fine light, the Swirlstone. . . . When the weather's clear, a big ship can see the flash of it over the horizon more than fifteen miles away."

"Cor!" Baker said.

"And that's what all this tower's for—all the thousands of tons of stone, and the machinery, and the stores, and the keepers, and everything—just to keep that light showing."

"What'd 'appen if it didn't show?" Baker said.

"The same thing that used to happen when there wasn't a tower. That's a long time ago now—but there were some shocking tragedies. Ships were always striking the rock. This reef lies in a very bad spot, you see—right in the approaches to Salmouth, just where a ship's likely to be when she's going into harbour. . . . Time and again, in the old days, a vessel would come safely back from right across the world, thousands and thousands of miles, and she'd be nearly home, and then on a thick night she'd strike this reef in the dark and down she'd go. Hundreds of wrecks there were—big ships and small ships. And hundreds of fine men drowned. . . . Yes, there've been some terrible disasters here. . . . But not now. Now they can all sail without fear, because the reef's lit and they know exactly where they are. . . ."

Baker was impressed. After a moment he said, "Reckon you like bein' a keeper, don't you?"

"I wouldn't have been one for forty-five years, son, if I hadn't."

"I wouldn't mind bein' one, in a way," Baker said. "Interestin', ain't it?"

"Oh, it's interesting, all right. . . . It gives you the feeling you're doing a bit of good in the world, too. Being useful. . . . It's better than thieving—or shooting people, the way Macey did . . ."

A shutter seemed to come down over Baker's face. The spell of the father-figure was broken.

"King didn't mean to shoot no one," Rosie said. "It was an accident. . . ."

Mitchell looked up from below. "The jury won't think that. . . . They'll say he's a murderer, and they'll be right. A cold-blooded murderer . . ."

"He's no murderer," Rosie said. "The gun went off. . . ." She was still loyal, but her voice had lost some of its fierce conviction.

Mitchell shook his head. "That's not what they said on the radio. They said it was deliberate. . . . Anyway, you can see it in his eyes. He's a callous brute. Isn't he always threatening to shoot us?—and don't you think he would, the moment we put a foot wrong . . .? I don't reckon he's got any ordinary human feelings."

"He has for me," Rosie said.

Robeson looked at her pityingly. "He's got a fine way of showing it, that's all I can say. Getting you into this mess. . . . The trouble with you two is that you've got into bad company—and you don't know how bad . . ."

Rosie sniffed. "You talk like all the rest of them. . . . Always preaching."

"I'm only trying to help you . . . I'd have thought a couple of bright kids like you would have had more sense than to get mixed up with toughs like Macey and Hines. . . . You could still do yourselves some good, you know, if you had a mind to."

"What d'you mean?" Baker said.

"I mean, if you helped us now, it would count in your favour. The other two will have to take what's coming to them—but you're different. You're both young—very young. You might easily be given another chance if you come over to our side."

Baker looked at Robeson in astonishment. "Against King, you mean?"

"That's right. . . . If you could help us to get that gun . . ."

"Not bloody likely," Baker said. "You must be barmy."

The swelling volume of Hines's radio announced his approach up the stairs from the service room. "Reckon it's your turn to watch the RT, Tommy," he said.

"Okay, Chris. . . ."

Hines looked around the horizon, found nothing to interest him, and descended the tower to join Lowe and Macey in the engine room. Lowe was cleaning and polishing the brass parts of the generators, apparently absorbed in his work. Macey was sitting on an upturned box a yard or two away from him, polishing his gun with equal diligence.

"Hi, Chris," he said. "Anythin' in sight up there yet?"

"Naow. . . . Not even a bit o' seaweed!"

"Too bad . . ." Macey held up the gun to the light. "Come up a treat, ain't it?"

Hines nodded. "Wish I got one."

"You ain't old enough, man. Gotta know what you're doin' . . ."

Lowe looked up from his polishing, "What kind of gun is it?"

"Luger," Macey said proudly. "Point three three eight automatic."

72

"What does that mean?"

"Don't you know, kid?"

"I've no idea."

"Well—point three eight, that's the size o' the bullet. Automatic means it goes on firin'.... Holds five bullets, see, in a magazine ...? Macey's expression came as near to a grin as he ever allowed it to. "One for each o' you geezers an' two to spare."

"I thought you used one."

"Yeah—but I shoved another in."

Lowe nodded. After a pause he said, "I hope it doesn't go off by mistake, that's all."

"Can't do that," Macey said. "Blimey, you don't know much about guns, do you?"

"I don't know anything about them."

"Well, it's got a safety-catch, see ..." Macey demonstrated. "Has to be cocked, too—like this ..." He cocked the automatic with his thumb. "Don't take 'alf a second.... Now I could shoot you dead, kid. Just a tiny pull on the trigger ..."

Lowe looked apprehensively into the barrel.

"Don't worry, I ain't goin' to.... Not yet, any rate."

"Where did you get the gun?" Lowe asked.

"Bought it off a school kid in a caff. Three an' a half nicker. It was his dad's, till his dad kicked the bucket.... Lovely job, ain't it?"

Hines grinned. "You got a licence for it, King?"

"'Course," Macey said. "Wouldn't 'ave a gun without no licence. Against the bleedin' law."

Hines did a half twirl on one foot. Lowe resumed his polishing. Hines said, "How long you been workin' in a light-house, kid?"

"About a year and a half," Lowe told him.

"Wouldn't no one give you a job nowhere else?"

"I didn't try anywhere else."

"Didn't *want* to come 'ere, did you?"

"Very much."

"Mean you like it?"

"Of course."

"More'n I would. . . . What you like about it?"

"I like the sea," Lowe said.

"You can 'ave it, boy. . . . Ain't nothin' to look at on the sea."

"I think there is," Lowe said mildly. He was anxious not to offend. "There are different colours, different lights. Sometimes the water's like silk—sometimes it's very wild. . . . And there's always something happening—ships in the distance, a school of porpoises leaping past, seals on the rocks, cormorants feeding, flotsam drifting by on the tide . . ."

"Cor, makes your blood race, don't it, King . . .!" Hines looked pityingly at the young keeper. "Don't you ever get cheesed off, kid?"

Lowe shook his head. "There's always plenty to do in the tower. . . . Anyway, I like a peaceful life."

Hines cackled. "Ain't very peaceful now, is it . . .?"

"No, it isn't."

"Don't you ever want a bird . . .? Don't you ever want to tear a piece off?"

"He's just a kid," Macey said. "He wouldn't know how."

"Lot o' ruddy monks, these geezers," Hines said. "Stuck out 'ere in the sea, thinkin' up chores to do. . . . Always on their ruddy knees. Bet you got prayer books, kid."

"Sometimes we need them," Lowe said.

"Any rate, why does there 'ave to be three of you . . .? Reckon one feller could ran this place on his own."

"You have to have three if you're going to set proper watches," Lowe said. "And in case of emergencies. . . . In the early days of lighthouses they tried to manage with two, but it didn't work."

"Why didn't it?"

"Oh, there were all sorts of problems. . . . The thing that really changed it was when a man died in one of the towers, and his fellow keeper kept the body in a room for weeks because he was afraid he might be charged with murder . . ."

"Cor!—hear that, King . . .? What a niff, eh!"

"There's always the chance of an accident, too—then you need all the hands you can get. A fire, for instance . . ." Lowe gave the

74

brass pipe he was working on a final rub, and got to his feet. "Would you like me to go and cook the dinner now, Macey?"

"I'll 'ave a nice bit o' roast turkey," Hines said.

"Okay, kid," Macey said. "On your way. . . ." He followed Lowe up the staircase, his gun held ready.

For the first time since the seizure of the tower, there was now no unfinished work for Robeson to worry about. The lantern was washed, the optic polished, the tower swept, the quota of rooms cleaned out. That afternoon the keepers all occupied themselves with their individual pursuits, much as they would have done if they'd had the place to themselves. Robeson settled down in a chair in the living-room to get on with a wool rug he was making. Lowe buried himself in a book. Mitchell, with a glance out of the window, said he thought he'd do a bit of fishing.

For the gang, who had virtually no interests, the time hung heavily. Only Macey, engrossed in his private fantasies, showed no outward sign of tedium. Baker was still maintaining the boat watch in the lantern room, but no longer with enthusiasm. There seemed to be no small boats at sea at all, and he stood disconsolately at the doors gazing out at nothing. Rosie was doing a stint beside the RT set, seeing little point in it and feeling lonely and utterly bored. Hines lounged in the living-room beside Macey, tapping his feet to some inner rhythm and chain-smoking. He'd found a large supply of cigarettes, the property of Mitchell, and was making free with them.

"What you readin', kid?" he asked Lowe. There was always some amusement to be got from badgering others.

"It's called *Typhoon*," Lowe said politely.

"Who's it by?"

"A man named Conrad."

"Never 'eard of 'im. . . . What's it like—any good?"

"It describes a storm very well," Lowe said.

"Let's 'ave a gander."

Lowe passed the book. Hines idly nicked over the pages.

"Some geezer's, been scribblin' in it," he said. "You put lines under this bit, kid?"

"No. . . . May I see?" Lowe took the book back and glanced at the heavily underscored phrase. It ran, 'The independent offspring of the ignoble freedom of the slums, full of disdain and hate for the austere servitude of the sea . . .'

He gave a faint smile. Mitchell, he knew, had been looking at the book the day before.

"It must have been some other keeper," he said. "These books go the round of the lighthouses."

"What's it mean?"

"It means that people living on land often don't like the sea," Lowe said tactfully.

Hines nodded. "That's what I been tellin' you, kid. . . ."

"If you'd like something to read yourself," Lowe said, "there's a whole box of books in the cupboard over there."

"Yeah, I seen 'em. . . . Just right for bloody monks."

"Some of them are thrillers."

"Seen them too," Hines said derisively. "Ain't you got no Mickey Spillane?"

"I don't think so."

"Cor, you geezers want to get with it . . ." Hines yawned, and got to his feet. For a moment he stood in front of the mirror, patting his back-swept hair. Then he looked at Robeson, who was quietly getting on with his rug.

"Like an old woman, King, ain't he . . .?" Hines stood watching, as Robeson drew small pieces of coïomred wool through holes in a square of canvas, using a special tool. "Wish I'd brought me knittin' . . .!"

Macey, sitting with the gun in his lap like an armed Buddha, said nothing.

"What you goin' to do with the rug when you finished it, Daddy-O?"

"Take it ashore with me," Robeson said.

"What's the pitcher goin' to be?"

"A ship."

"Ain't very chatty, are you?"

"No," Robeson said.

"Too ruddy busy, ain't you . . .? Always ruddy busy. . . ." Hines's glance fell on the tool that Robeson was using. "Blimey, that's sharp, ain't it . . .? Say, King, d'you reckon we oughter let Daddy-O 'ave a tool like that? Might give 'im ideas. . . . Reckon we should take it away an' put it somewhere safe."

"Leave 'im alone," Macey said. "I got him covered."

Hines gave the box of wool a kick, upsetting it. "Pardon me!" he said.

He went and fiddled with the radio, but couldn't find anything that pleased him. "Cor—how much longer we goin' to be here. King?"

"You know how long," Macey said. "Till we see a boat."

Mitchell was leaning out over the gallery rail, looking up at the wind vane on the cupola. Beside him on the gallery there was a large canvas kite on a metal frame. A fickle breeze ruffled the sea below.

There was a step in the lantern room behind him and Rosie drifted out. She'd just taken over the watch from Baker. "Hallo," she said amiably.

Mitchell turned. "Hallo. . . ." He didn't approve of Rosie, but she was so pretty he couldn't bring himself to be uncivil to her.

She looked at the kite. "You going to fly that?"

"No. . . . The wind's dropped too much—and what there is is all over the place."

"You like flying kites?"

"I like fishing with them."

"Fishing . . .?"

"It's the way we usually fish. . . . Down on the rocks it's not often calm enoughs."

"What do you do, then?"

"Well—you see this long tail the kite's got—this cord here . . ." Mitchell showed her. "It's long enough to reach the water. . . . When you're going to fish, you tie ten or a dozen hooks to the last few

77

feet of it, and bait them, and then let the kite fly out on its line. The hooks go down into the water and after a bit, if you're lucky, you catch something."

"It don't sound too easy," Rosie said.

"No, it's not easy—but it's good sport. . . . If the wind's strong, you have to belay round the rail or the line'll take the skin off your fingers. . . . You've got to play the kite, too—it takes a bit of knack. You've got to let it out till it's hovering over the right spot, and then drop it and let the current take the bait, so the fish think it's natural."

"I bet I couldn't do it," Rosie said, "You ever catch much?"

"I got a twelve-pound bass just before Christmas," Mitchell told her. "Lovely fish—biggest bass I ever saw. Lasted us two days. . . . It's a bit late in the season for bass now, though." He eyed her thoughtfully. Out of Macey's company, she seemed a different girl. "Next time I have a go," he said, "maybe you'd like to watch."

"I wouldn't mind," Rosie said. "Be something to look at, wouldn't it . . .? There ain't much else," She turned towards the door.

"Have you thought any more about what the skipper said?" Mitchell asked.

"What did he say?"

"He said you could do yourself a bit of good by helping us."

"No, I ain't."

"Well, it's a pity . . ." Mitchell looked at her curiously. "What does your dad think about you getting in with this lot?"

Rosie gave a scornful laugh. "If I knew who me dad was, I'd ask him," she said—and went inside.

She sat down at the foot of the optic ladder and made up her face. It was about the most comforting thing she could find to do and she did it a dozen times a day. She had to go on wearing the same clothes, but at least she could change her face a bit. . . .

Presently Baker came up the stairs. Rosie was surprised to see him. "Ain't you s'posed to be watching the telephone. Tommy . . .?"

"That's okay," Baker said, "Robeson's on the blower to his

coastguard pal. . . . He don't 'alf sound funny when he's talkin'.
. . . Kind o' choked up . . ."

"So would you be if someone was shoving a gun into you,"
Rosie said.

"I guess so . . ." For a moment, Baker stood silently beside her.
"No sign of a boat, Rosie?"

"No—you can see for yourself. . . . And if you ask me, there ain't
going to be one. I reckon Mitchell was right."

Baker gazed around. "It'll soon be dark," he said.

"Yes . . . I hate it when it's dark. Worse than the daytime."

Baker nodded.

"Wish we was back in Salmouth," Rosie said. She looked towards
the land. Lights were just beginning to show on Sheep Head.

"Don't see how we're ever goin' to be able to go back there,"
Baker said. "Not after what's 'appened."

"Well, some other place, then. . . . Some place with a nice bright
caff and a juke-box and lots of boys to dance with and something
tasty to eat. . . . Know what I'd like, Tommy?"

"No—what?"

"Fish and chips."

"Me too, Rosie."

"If we was in a place like that we could go to the pictures, if
we wanted to. . . . And there'd be shops and lights and crowds on
the pavements. . . . Bit of life. . . . It's like being dead here."

Baker sighed. "Oh, well, I 'spect King'll get us out of it pretty
soon. . . ."

"I don't know how," Rosie said.

Mitchell switched the light on as he passed through the lantern
room and went on down to set the generator going before joining
the others. Presently, Rosie and Baker went down too.

Macey's eyes brightened as Rosie entered the living-room. "Say,
you're lookin' a treat to-night, chick."

"If I am, it's a wonder," Rosie said.

Macey stretched out an arm and drew her on to his lap. He
lowered his voice a little. "What about a spot o' love, Rosie?"

"Don't be daft . . ."

"Why not, there ain't no one in the bedroom. . . . Let's have a bit o' fun."

Hines sniggered. "Go on, Rosie, you know you'll like it."

"You shut your trap," Macey said. "Come on, Rosie, don't give me the old moody . . ."

"It's too public," Rosie said.

"It ain't public up there."

"Please, King, I wish you wouldn't, not now . . . I don't feel like it, honest."

"Aw, don't be like that, Rosie. . . . You're my girl, ain't you?"

She struggled a little.

Mitchell said, "Why don't yon let her alone, you big ape?"

Robeson put a restraining hand on his arm. "Easy, Mitch . . .!"

"You better come, Rosie," Macey said. "You better do what I say . . ."

"They all know . . ."

"Cor, you got fussy, ain't you?"

"Let me go, King, you're hurting . . ."

Hines said, "Go on, King, you take her. Do your stuff, boy. . . . Better gimme your gun, though. Might need it."

Macey loosed his hold of Rosie. "Got your knife, Chris, ain't you?"

"That ain't enough against them two geezers. Not if they ain't tied."

"Tie 'em," Macey said.

"Blimey, King, we goin' to eat soon—it ain't worth it. . . . Any rate, what about the kid?"

"Where is he?"

"I dunno—wanderin' around somewhere. . . . Look, why don't you jus' lend me your gun, King. Just lend it to me. . . . I won't hurt it."

Macey shook his head. "I ain't partin' with this gun for no one, mate. . . . Okay, Rosie, you can keep your passion killers on. Maybe later, eh . . .?"

After supper that evening Macey put on Lowe's cap as well as his uniform jacket and went for a stroll round the gallery on his own. He liked it up there, especially in the early morning and at night. He was easy in his mind now, for the tension of the day was over. The keepers were safely tied up, the watches had been arranged with Hines and Baker, and Macey could relax. . . .

The night was mild, and very dark. Looking down, all he could see of the water was a thin line of foam where the rocks gashed the sea. There was almost no wind. The only sound was the faint hum of the optic turning on its rollers. Above his head, six pairs of beams circled and stretched to the distant horizon. Each time the spokes revolved, the prisms criss-crossed his jacket with a rainbow spectrum.

Macey looked out from his quarter-deck and felt pretty good. He'd got everything organised very well now. It had been a bright idea of his to free the keepers during the day so that they could get on with their jobs and keep the place decent for him. The new routine had gone smoothly that day and would go even more smoothly to-morrow. The food had been much better since young Lowe had started to do the cooking. . . . Yes, things were fine in his domain. Macey even felt good that the light was working properly—the tower wouldn't have been the same without it. . . . He liked to see the light, and know that his arrangements were keeping it going. It was really *his* light, now. . . .

Of course, there were a few minor annoyances. . . .Mitchell, always ready to talk out of turn and make trouble. . . . Rosie being difficult. . . . And mutterings among his henchmen about not getting away. . . . Still, he could deal with them all right. He certainly didn't share their discontents. *He* hadn't felt bored that day. Looking out now at the pinpoints of light on distant Sheep Head, he felt none of Rosie's nostalgia for the shore. He preferred to have a lighthouse. . . .

Presently he heard someone moving around in the service room, and went down. It was Hines. He was amusing himself by drawing a female figure on the wall with a blue pencil. A slightly obscene figure, which made him snicker.

"How's that for a nice pair o' top-uns?" he said, standing back to admire his work.

Macey's face darkened. "Who said you could do that . . .? Clean it off!"

"What d'you mean, clean it off? I ain't even finished it yet."

"You 'eard me. . . . Spoilin' the look o' the place."

"Cor, I ain't spoilin' nothin'. . . . Makin' it nicer, King. What's wrong with a few pitchers?"

"Clean it, I said. . . . You ain't fit for a decent place like this. Messin' up the walls. . . ."

Hines said in a grumbling tone, "It's okay for you, King, you got a bird. . . . I ain't even got a pin-up. Now if I 'ad Rosie. . . ."

"Belt up, will you . . .!" Macey took a menacing step towards him. "You lookin' for a flash, mate?"

Hines shrank back. "'Course not, King . . ."

"Then stop rabbitin' an' get that wall cleaned the way it was before."

"Okay," Mines said, "okay."

Chapter Four

Outwardly, there was nothing in the start of the third day at the tower to indicate any weakening in Macey's authority.

The night had passed quietly. Hines had carried out his share of the watches with no more than his usual murmurings about lack of sleep. Baker, as always, had been willing and amenable. Rosie had gone early to bed and given no trouble.

In the morning, things were still quiet. The keepers appeared to have resigned themselves to their situation and did whatever Macey said without demur. Mitchell switched off the light and generator half an hour after sunrise, when he was told to. Robeson, forced by the gun to accompany Macey on his morning promenade round the gallery, showed no open hostility. Lowe cooked an excellent breakfast of bacon and sausage for seven, and washed up afterwards as a matter of course. Baker went off obediently after breakfast to resume the boat watch over the still tranquil sea. Rosie looked a bit glum when Macey told her to go and sit by the RT, but she went all the same.

During the morning, the keepers carried out the routine chores of the light with their customary efficiency. Macey encouraged their efforts, and for an hour or two the tower fairly hummed with activity. Robeson, perched on the top of the step-ladder, washed all the lantern panes, inside and out, and afterwards polished the optic with loving care, breaking off only to make his report to the shore when the time came. Mitchell thoroughly cleaned the living-room and the bedroom and swept the hundred steps. Lowe humped coal for the stove on his broad back, and pumped water, and greased the generator, and baked the day's bread. Busy as beavers, they all were, Macey thought. Real gluttons for work. It was a pleasure to see them at it....

He swaggered among them like an overseer, wearing Lowe's jacket as his badge of office, always putting his cap on when he went out on the gallery with one of them, always holding his gun at the ready. His distinction, his superior status, was more than ever marked now by the fact that he alone was shaved. Hines hadn't bothered, and the keepers hadn't been allowed to, and Baker had grown no more than a blond fuzz. A scruffy lot, Macey thought—and for the moment it suited him. He could always make them smarten up when he felt like it....

He sensed no change in the ordered atmosphere as the morning wore on, but it was there—mostly out of his sight.

At a few minutes after eleven Rosie handed over the RT watch to Hines in accordance with Macey's instructions and went up to the lantern room where she was supposed to take over the boat watch from Baker.

"Want the binoculars?" he asked her.

She shook her head. "Never could see through them prop'ly.... Anyway, what is there to see?"

"Nothing," Baker said. "Just water."

Rosie flopped down on the optic ladder. "I ain't going to bother any more, Tommy.... I'm sick of looking out there."

"Cor—King'll 'ave something to say if you don't."

"Who cares?"

"But s'pose something comes—an' you don't see it?"

"Nothing ain't going to come here," Rosie said. "Why should it?—what's there, to come for ...? Nothing won't come till the big boat comes.... Wish it was coming to-day!"

"They'll only stick us in the nick, Rosie."

"What if they do ...? I tell you, I'm fed up with being here. Fed right up. Nothing to do, nowhere to go.... And all this stone closing in on you.... If I have to stay here for four more weeks I'll go crazy, honest I will. I'll start screaming ..."

"That won't do no good," Baker said.

"It'll do *me* good . . .! Four weeks, Tommy—just think of it. All them days . . ."

Baker gave a gloomy nod. "Don't see what we can do about it, though. . . ." He shuffled uneasily. "You really not goin' to keep watch, Rosie?"

"Not any more . . . I told you—I'm sick of it."

"Like me to do it for you?"

"Suit yourself."

Baker looked out. There was still nothing visible on the winter sea but far-away wisps of smoke. Presently he shrugged, and went off downstairs.

The service room door was ajar. Hines was lolling beside the RT set with his mouth slightly open and a vacuous expression on his face. Baker paused for a moment—then went on down. He didn't feel like talking to Hines just now. He felt more like getting some exercise if he could. He passed Mitchell on one of the landings, busy with a dustpan and broom, and continued down the spiral to the entrance door. Perhaps he'd be able to have a scramble over the rocks. . . . But when he looked out he saw that the rising tide had already begun to wash over them. And the set-off itself was no better to walk round than the gallery. . . . It was true what Rosie had said, there was nowhere to go in this place. It was all right for one day, specially, when it was all new and interesting—but you came to hate it. Baker couldn't think how the keepers stuck it. He longed for a street, where he could step out briskly. His body craved for action. . . .

Dejectedly, he climbed back up the tower to the sitting-room. He found Lowe alone there. Macey, he learned, had gone to the engine room with Robeson. There was a smell of newly-baked bread in the air—but Baker didn't find it particularly appetising. There was nothing in the cramped life of the tower to give you an appetite. . . . He saw that Lowe had the window open and was doing something there. Lowe was always doing something. He always managed to look fairly cheerful, too. . . . Baker joined him at the window. A seagull was hovering outside, catching bits of food that Lowe was tossing to it. Baker stood watching. When Lowe stopped throwing food the bird came in on to the ledge and squawked.

Baker grinned. "Tame, ain't he?"

"Yes," Lowe said, "Charlie's tame all right. He's a regular. . . . He's been here every day for weeks."

"I ain't seen him before."

"He was around yesterday. . . . He missed his meal, but that wasn't his fault. . . . Nor mine."

Baker picked up a wire-and-wood contraption that was lying in the window embrasure. "What's this—a perch?"

"That's right."

"What you goin' to do with it?"

"Fix it up outside," Lowe said. "It's from the Bird Society. They make them specially. . . ."

"Is it just for seagulls?"

"No, it's for any bird that happens to drop in. We get all sorts—lots of migrating ones in the season. They get tired sometimes, and the tower makes a good resting place. . . ."

He threw a final crust. "There you are, Charlie—that's your lot . . ." The gull snapped it up, hovered for a moment as the window was closed, and then flew off like an arrow over the sea.

Baker watched it sadly. "Wish I had wings," he said.

Mitchell glanced in through the service room door on his way up to the gallery. Hines saw him, and called out, "Where you off to, bright boy?"

Mitchell carried on, as though he hadn't heard.

Hines whipped out his knife and leapt for the door. "I'm talkin' to you, Mitchell. Ain't you got on ears?"

Mitchell stopped. "I m going to get some fresh air. Any objection?"

"Maybe I have an' maybe I haven't. . . . Any rate, you better keep a civil tongue." Hines went closer to Mitchell. "You don't like me, do you?"

"No."

"An' I don't like you, see."

Mitchell said nothing, hoping the pureile exchange would end there. But it didn't. Hines was bored, and needling Mitchell was a relief.

"You geezers ain't exactly chatty, are you . . .? Doncher ever talk to each other?"

"Sometimes."

"I ain't heard you much."

"There isn't much to say just now."

"S'pose you're such good pals you can read each other's minds?"

"I think we can," Mitchell said grimly.

"An' I can read yours. . . . You'd like to get hold o' this knife, wouldn't you?"

"Not particularly."

"Bet you would . . .! But you ain't goin' to. . . ." Hines groped in the cavity of his mind for a fresh topic. "I can tell you this, bright boy—I wouldn't 'ave your life."

"I'm sure you wouldn't."

"Killin' time, that's all you do. . . . Messin' around."

"We work." Mitchell said. "Why don't you try it?"

Hines cackled. "Not ruddy likely. . . . You won't catch me sweepin' a hundred flippin' steps. I got me dignity to think of, see. . . ."

Mitchell made no reply. Hines suddenly lost interest in chivvying him, and let him go.

Mitchell went on up, fuming. Robeson had urged him not to let himself be provoked, but it was getting harder.

Hines went back to the RT set and sat there, gnawing his nails and thinking what he might be doing if he wasn't stuck in the tower. He felt almost crazy with tedium. Ashore, now, there was always something to do—a bit of mischief to get up to, a job to be planned, money to fling around, a girl to mess about with in the back of a car. If there was nothing else, you could always do a bit of damage and let off steam that way. . . . Here you couldn't even do that without having Macey jump on you. Hines seethed with frustration and resentment. Those bloody keepers!—going on almost as though nothing had happened. Behaving as though they still ran the show. Sticking together like one man. Not even bothering to talk, they were so sure of themselves. Just waiting. . . . And Macey, sitting around with his gun all day, giving his orders, looking pleased with himself. . . .

Hines stabbed his knife down hard in the table. Twenty-five more bloody days—and then the nick . . .!

Midday dinner brought only a temporary break in the monotony. An hour after it was over, the hopeless boredom of the morning had settled on the gang more firmly than ever. The fact that, by contrast, the keepers still seemed to have no difficulty in occupying themselves, merely made things worse. Lowe was finishing the bracket for his bird-perch, apparently quite absorbed. Robeson and Mitchell were playing a game of cribbage with every outward sign of concentration. Rosie and Baker were following the cards, but with little interest. Rosie had a sullen, shut-in look on her face. Baker was wondering if he ought to tell Macey that the boat watch was as good as over, but felt worried about the storm he'd bring down on his head. Hines was smoking cigarette after cigarette and not talking to anyone. His silence was so unusual as to be almost sinister. Macey sat aloof, clasping his gun, unaware of the explosive dissatisfaction around him.

It was about three o'clock when Hines suddenly said, "King—I been thinkin'."

Macey gazed unemotionally at his lieutenant. "You'll strain yourself, mate."

"Aw, cut it out, King. I got a good idea."

"About what?"

"About 'ow we can get away from the perishin' dump."

Baker and Rosie were alert at once.

"I bet you ain't," Macey said. "Doin' all we can already."

"Maybe he's got a new idea," Rosie said.

Baker nodded eagerly. "Let's hear it, King, any rate."

Macey shrugged. "Okay—let's 'ave it, then."

"Well," Hines began, "we still got good weather, ain't we? Calm as anything outside. Right now, anyone could step out of a boat on to the rocks easy—be just a doddle. . . . I reckon if the relief boat was to come out now, they wouldn't 'ave no trouble at all. It'd be the one time in twenty Daddy-O was talkin' about."

Macey's face was blank, "Don't see what you're gettin' at, Chris. . . . The relief boat *ain't* comin'—so what's it all about?"

"We could easy make it come if we wanted to," Hines said. "Any time. . . . All we gotta do is call up on the blower."

"What'd we want to do that for?"

"Because if it came out we could take over the motor boat, same as you said."

"Blimey, Chris, we turned that idea in right at the start."

"Yeah, because we reckoned the geezers on the tender would see what we was up to. . . . But if we could work it so the tender come out in the dark, we could nick the boat an' scarper an' no one wouldn't 'ave a suss what was happenin'."

Baker gave a quick nod. "That's right, King. . . . Reckon Chris has got somethin' there."

"More than I do," Macey said. "How could we work it so the tender got here in the dark? How could we know they wouldn't come in daylight?"

"Easy," Hines said. "Tell 'em it was urgent. . . .Don't you see?—we'd make Daddy-O ring up an' say there's been a bad accident—a big fire—somethin' like that. He'd ring up as soon as it got dark—an' tell 'em he needed help bad. . . . Then they'd be out here like a bullet."

Macey grunted. "Well, maybe they would. Maybe we could get 'em out in the dark. . . . But what if they didn't land on the rock? We couldn't be sure about that. What if the wind got up a bit an' they 'appened to think the breeches-buoy thing would be easier. . . . Then we'd be right up the ruddy creek. Can't see Rosie gettin' down a rope in the dark. Can't see any of us doin' it, come to that."

"We wouldn't have to," Hines said impatiently. "Don't you see, King, they'd be forced to land on the rock this time because there wouldn't be no other way for 'em. . . . There's been injuries in the accident, see. There's been burns. So there ain't no one to throw 'em a rope. That's what Daddy-O'll say. They gotta come quick an' lay on a rescue all on their own. . . . Man, it's a cinch."

Macey shook his head. "It wouldn't work."

"Why wouldn't it work . . .? I can see it all happenin'. We tie these geezers up, an' soon as we see the lights o' the tender comin' we all go down to the rocks, leavin' the entrance door open behind us. We wait there in the dark, an' after a bit the motor boat comes in close an' ties up. The geezers in it ain't sussin' nothin' an' they ain't worryin' about the place bein' all quiet an' no one around because o' what they've heard about the injuries. . . . Then you an' me steps out with the gun an' the knife an' puts the frighteners on 'em, an' Rosie an' Tommy climbs into the boat, an' we're off—leavin' the geezers behind on the rock. . . . I tell you, King, it can't go wrong."

"That's what you think, mate. They'd probably have a searchlight shinin' on us from the tender."

"What, quarter of a mile away . . .! If there was a searchlight it'd more likely be on the motor boat—an' that could help us if we was careful. Help the geezers to see the gun!"

"You don't know where the searchlight'd be," Macey said. "Just guessin', that's what you're doin'. . . . Any rate, the blokes on the tender'd know there was something wrong soon as they heard the motor boat clearin' off. An' they got wireless, ain't they? We'd have a proper reception committee waitin' for us on the shore."

"Cor, King, they wouldn't know what had happened—they wouldn't know it was us. . . . An' how could there be a reception committee when we wouldn't even know ourselves where we was goin' to land . . .? Man, yon ain't chicken, are you?"

"You watch out who you're callin' chicken, Chris. . . . I got a responsibility, that's all."

"Well, I say we gotta take a chance," Hines said. "Things is just right now, with the weather an' everything, an' we gotta take advantage. . . . I reckon it's now or never. What you say. Tommy?"

"I'm with you, Chris," Baker said, "Gotta do something."

"That's right," Hines said. "Anything's better than stayin' an' rottin' here—sittin' on our fannies, waitin' for 'em to come out in three or four weeks an' take us all off to the nick. . . . What's the sense in that, King?"

"There's a lot of sense in it if a small boat comes in close," Macey said. "Something with just a couple o' geezers in it, maybe. We'll be able to take over an' get away easy then."

"There ain't goin' to be no small boat," Hines said. "Three days we been watchin', an' not a bleedin' thing. . . . Do you reckon there's goin' to be anything come along, Tommy?"

Baker shook his head.

"You reckon there is, Rosie?"

"Be a miracle," she said.

"There you are, King—it's three to one."

Macey appeared to consider. Then he delivered judgment. "Well, we ain't goin' to risk it."

"You mean we just goin' to wait. . .?" Hines's tone was disbelieving.

"That's right, Chris—till some boat shows up. Gotta be one some time. . . . Anyway, what's wrong with waitin'?—that's what I'd like to know. We're cosy here, ain't we? We got all we need."

"You speak for yourself," Rosie said.

"Well, we got most things. . . . We got fire an' shelter an' a place to doss in. We got food an' water an' plenty o' snout. . . . Dunno what you're all beefin' about. We can hold out for months if we have to . . ."

Hines gave him a startled look. "What you mean?"

"I mean, I been thinkin' too," Macey said complacently. "We got a fortress here, mate. All we gotta do is bar that entrance door an' no one can't get in. They can send all the relief boats they want, but if we don't open up for 'em they'll just have to go away again, see."

"What, an' leave us here?" Baker said.

"That's right, Tommy."

"'Course they wouldn't leave us," Hines said scornfully. "They'd send a ruddy helicopter an' drop someone on the gallery."

"Not if I was up there with the gun, they wouldn't. We could stop 'em—we could hold out. We got hostages, don't forget. Three of 'em. It'd be like in the nick when the lags grab the guv'nor—no one couldn't do nothin' to us. . . . Trouble with you lot is, you ain't got no spirit. . . . I tell you, we got everything for a good fight. 'The Battle of the Swirlstone'—that's what the papers'd call it. Can't you see the headlines?—big as your fist. ' "King" Macey Defies the Navy' . . . ' "King" Macey says "No Surrender" ' . . . We'll be a legend, mate. We'll be famous. . . . Folks'll be readin' about us in a hundred years."

Hines stared at him. "You're bats," he said. "So help me, you're a bleedin' nut case. . . . An' to think that all this time we been leavin' everything to you!"

"Don't see you got anything to complain about," Macey said. "All alive an' well, ain't yon? None o' you ain't in the nick. Reckon I been runnin' things pretty good."

"Oh, no, you ain't . . ." Hines's resentment, repressed for days, suddenly burst out in a torrent of accusation. "It was you what got us into all this, right at the start. I told you we shouldn't 'ave done that job in the fog, I said it was risky, but no, you had to do it. . . . Then you used your shooter when there wasn't no call. . . . Then you ran the ruddy boat into that post an' damn' near drowned us. . . . I tell you, mate, we wouldn't be here at all if it wasn't for you. . . . An' now, to crown the lot, you want to ruddy well stay here . . .! What's more, I know why."

Macey stirred dangerously. "Well—why?"

"Man, I oughter 'ave sussed you long ago. I can see it all now. You just been leadin' us up the garden, ain't you? You never did think there was goin' to be no yacht or small boat, did you? Just talk, it was, to keep us quiet. You didn't ever want to get away. You was plannin' all the time to stay here an' shoot it out, because you know they'll bloody well top you when they get hold of you. . . . Well, they won't top me, mate, because I didn't do no shootin', an' they won't top Tommy nor Rosie. If they nab us, I'll get a laggin' an' they'll get a stretch, an' that's all. . . . So I'm ready to take a chance, see, an' I reckon these kids are too."

"You finished?" Macey said.

Hines looked at Baker, as though seeking support. "Yeah. . . . What you got to say about it?"

"This is what I got to say . . ." Macey cocked the gun and levelled it at Hines. "If you ain't tired o' life, mate, you're goin' to do what I tell you. . . . I'm 'King' here, an' don't you forget it. . . . You're goin' to stay in this tower an' you're goin' to like it, an' that's all there is to it. I got enough trouble already with these geezers. You start givin' trouble too, an' I'll ruddy well do you. I ain't kiddin'. . . . Now belt up, will you!"

There was a tense silence. Hines had shrunk back into his chair. Baker's face was wooden. Rosie looked pertified.

After a moment, Hines said, "You got me wrong, King—I wasn't tryin' to start nothin'. . . . Only makin' a suggestion. . . ."

Robeson took his pipe out of his pocket, and lit it. His face, in the flame of the match, looked very tired.

The quarrel had seared everyone. After two comparatively quiet and peaceful days, violence was in the air again. The atmosphere in the tower remained tense all afternoon. Macey sat in a brooding silence, moving only for Robeson's routine call to the shore. He had reasserted his authority without any trouble, but it didn't give him much satisfaction. He wasn't at all sure that in a crisis he could count any longer on the loyalty of his troops. They might have to be driven into the battle when it came, not led. Macey felt bitter, deserted, and hated every face.

Hines mood was even uglier. He drifted around the tower with the scowl of a beaten rebel, consumed with resentment, ripe for any safe mischief. Rosie and Baker, appalled by the prospect of an indefinite stay in the lighthouse, knowing in their hearts that Hines had been right about Macey, found what comfort they could in each other's company. The keepers had as little to say as Macey himself. For them, the future had become even more unpredictable.

As dusk fell, Mitchell went out to switch on the generator and the light. Afterwards, he took a turn round the gallery. He stayed there for a few minutes, gazing out over the sea, mulling over the situation. When he re-entered the lantern room he found Hines

93

standing at the foot of the optic ladder, toying with his flick-knife and, by the look in his eye, plotting something.

"What are you up to?" Mitchell said.

"Just thinkin', bright boy.... Just thinkin' how the relief boat could be on its way by now if we'd sent that RT message like I wanted."

"Well—you heard what Macey said."

"Him!" Hines spat on the floor. "The flash bastard! Who does he think he is, shoutin' the odds! ... He's crackers, that baron."

"He's got the gun."

"He ain't got the brains, though."

"You don't need brains to shoot."

"I ain't scared," Hines said. He jerked his head towards the optic. "You keep any spare lamps for that gadget?"

"Of course."

"Thought you might.... Wouldn't be much good if the whole thing got busted, though, would they?" Hines looked around. The iron bar that Baker had carried for a short time and then discarded, was leaning against the wall. "Reckon it wouldn't be hard to bust it with that.... Then the relief boat would come, wouldn't it? Come pretty quick, I reckon, if the light had gone out.... Then King wouldn't have no choice—he'd have to do what I said."

"He'd kill you."

Hines gave the keeper a cunning look. "Not if he thought you done it, bright boy."

"He'd know I'd never smash the light."

"Would he, though ...? I been thinkin' about that, too.... I'd say you went for me, see. I'd say I was up there on the platform, havin' a quiet dekko, an' you rushed up with that iron bar an' took a swipe at me an' missed an' hit the ruddy glass.... Crackin' idea, ain't it?" Hines picked up the bar.

"Don't be a damned fool...." Mitchell took a step towards him.

The knife blade flashed in Hines's left hand. "Watch it, Mitchell ...! You come near me an' I'll slit you up."

Mitchell stopped. "You'd never get away with it.... Macey would never believe you."

94

"'Course he would. . . . He knows you been wantin' a bundle ever since we come here. Tried to grab his gun, didn't you, that first night. An' you been lookin' for a chance ever since. . . ." Hines grinned. He was enjoying the keeper's agitation. If he couldn't take it out of Macey, he could take it out of Mitchell. "Any rate, if the light was busted he'd need me around, see, to help him when the boat came. . . . He wouldn't dare shoot." Hines swung the bar a little, testing its weight.

Mitchell glanced in the direction of the staircase, wondering if Macey would hear a shout. . . . Hines read his mind.

"You let out one squeak, bright boy, an' I'll carve you. . . ."

Mitchell's hands clenched. Hines might not mean what he'd said about the light, but he looked as though he did. He had a foot on the ladder now. . . . Mitchell around in desperation. His eye fell on the metal loud hailer. . . .

"Reckon I will bust it," Hines said, grasping the rail.

Mitchell dived for the loud hailer and hurled himself on Hines, reckless of consequences. He hardly felt the knife rip into him. He saw a head within striking distance and brought down the edge of the loud hailer on it with all his strength. Hines gave one scream as the weapon descended—then crashed to the floor.

In the living-room, the scream and the thud brought Macey to his feet. He rushed out and up the spiral staircase, with Baker and Robeson at his heels and Lowe and Rosie following behind.

In the lantern room he paused for a second, taking in the scene. Hines unconscious on the floor. Mitchell, with blood pouring from his left arm, still grasping the loud hailer. . . .

Mitchell started to explain. "He was going to smash the light . . ."

"Like hell," Macey said. Now the pent-up violence of the day could find release in him, too. He raised his gun and shot Mitchell squarely through the forehead.

Chapter Five

As the echoes of the shot died away Macey stepped farther into the room, covering the staircase to stop any rush. But there wasn't any rush Robeson, emerging behind Baker, stood for a moment rooted, staring, unable to believe that what he had feared all along had actually happended. Then, with a groan, he crossed the floor and bent over Mitchell. One glance was sufficient to tell him the keeper was dead. He straightened up and turned on Macey. His lips moved, as though in execration, but no sound escaped them. The only sound came from Rosie, who suddenly let out a wail. Macey pointed the gun at Robeson and motioned to him to get back down the stairs. "You too, Rosie. . . ." Crying bitterly, Rosie descended. Robeson went down after her, slowly, like a very old man.

Macey picked up the iron bar from the floor and handed it to Baker. "Go an' keep an eye on the blower, Tommy. . . . An' tell Rosie to stop that bloody snivellin'. . . ." Baker took the bar in a dazed way and went off without a word.

Macey looked round for Lowe. The young keeper had disappeared. "Hi, kid . . .!" he called down the stairs.

He waited impatiently. In a few moments, Lowe returned. His face was chalk white. What he'd seen of the shambles in the lantern room had almost turned his stomach.

"Need you to 'elp me," Macey said.

Lowe nodded mechanically. The sudden burst of violence, the fearful shock of Mitchell's death, had left him without any will of his own.

"Better get Chris into the bedroom," Macey said.

Lowe looked down at the unconscious man, at the growing pool of blood around his head. The thought crossed his mind that perhaps Hines ought not to be moved. The wound at the crown of his head was very ugly—he appeared to be seriously hurt. . . . But if Macey wanted it that way. . . .

"Lift him up," Macey said, "Bring him to the stairs."

Fighting his nausea, Lowe raised Hines on to his shoulder in a fireman's lift. "If you like," he said, "I can carry him down on my own. . . . Shall I?"

Macey nodded. "Okay . . ."

Lowe crossed to the stairs and backed carefully down the two flights with his burden. Macey followed him to the bedroom. There, Lowe laid Hines on one of the bunks. There was blood everywhere now—on the pillow, on Lowe's jersey, on the floor and the stairs. . . .

Macey was quite unaffected. "Right," he said. "Now you an' Robeson better get rid o' that stiff upstairs. . . . Shove 'im in the sea . . ."

In silence, Lowe and Robeson eased and carried Mitchell's body down the length of the tower. Macey, with the gun, followed close behind them—an evil presence that robbed them of any desire to speak.

In Robeson's mind, grief was uppermost—grief for the loss of a tried and loyal colleague whose face he wouldn't see again. Grief which for the moment seemed to leave no place for anger. Grief made worse, too, by self-reproach. If someone was going to be killed in any case, it would have been better to make a fight of it from the start. At the cost of a man, they could probably have got the gun. . . . And if someone was to be killed, it should have been himself. It shouldn't have been Mitch. . . .

Lowe was still hardly capable of consecutive thought. He felt the loss, too, but for the moment other emotions were stronger. He had suffered an appalling shock. He could scarcely believe in the reality of such cold-blooded killing. It would take time for his mind to adjust to the shattering experience. Overwhelmed with horror and fearful of the future, he felt more than ever thankful that Robeson was around. . . .

They stopped in the store room for the last sombre rites. Robeson found a square of tarpaulin behind the wall of paint tins and spread it out on the floor. Lowe helped him to lift Mitchell's body on to it. Robeson laid some bits of iron ballast on the dead man's chest, and together they wrapped the tarpaulin round him and lashed up the grim parcel with rope.

The body was heavier now, but the entrance door was near. Lowe unbarred and opened it. Robeson tied a stout line round the body and the two men lowered it to the set-off. Then they followed it down. The tide was at half-ebb, the sea quiet. The night was very dark, but Lowe had brought a torch. Robeson undid the rope, and between them they carried Mitchell to the side of the set-off where, a few feet out, they knew the water was deep even at the lowest tides.

They rested for a moment. Then Robeson said, "All right, Jim. . . . Let's get it over."

They took the body by the head and the feet, swung it between them to gain momentum, and at a word from Robeson heaved it out under the set-off railing. It seemed unceremonious, but there was no other way of making sure it would reach deep water. There was a splash from below. Lowe shone his torch down. Nothing was to be seen but a little foam.

"God rest him," Robeson said. Then, as though he felt something more was needed, he added quietly, "He was a good keeper, Jim. . . . It was for the light he did it. . . .?

Rosie and Baker were waiting in the living-room. Baker had done what he could for Hines, which wasn't much. Now he was sitting by the stove, pale and silent. Rosie was staring out of the window. Her eyes were red, but she'd stopped crying. As Macey came in with the others, she rounded on him.

"What did you have to kill him for?"

"Because he went for Chris," Macey said.

"You didn't have to shoot him. He hadn't got no gun. . . . You're always shooting people."

"Aw, put a cork in it, will you. . . . Mitchell asked for it, didn't he—startin' a bundle like that. . . ."

"He didn't start it . . ."

Macey shrugged. "Any rate, he shouldn't have hit Chris. . . . I had to make an example, see. Next thing, we'd 'ave these two geezers goin' for us."

Baker said, "Chris looks pretty bad, King."

"Yeah?"

"You reckon he'll be okay?"

"'Course he will. . . . We'll stick a bandage on 'im."

"I done that," Baker said.

Macey gave a grudging nod. "That's all right, then."

"Well, I dunno . . ." Baker still looked anxious.

A corner of Lowe's shocked mind suddenly began to work again. There might be a chance for them here. . . . He looked at Robeson. Robeson's face was blank. The old man's thoughts were evidently still with Mitchell. Lowe looked at Macey, at the gun. He feared the gun more than ever now—but for the moment Macey's destructive spasm seemed to be over. Lowe spoke up.

"If you ask me," he said, "Hines's skull is fractured."

"I didn't ask you," Macey snarled.

"Anyway, I think it is. . . . He ought to go to hospital."

"You don't know nothin' about it, kid."

"I know a little. . . . It's the way he's breathing."

"He's lucky to be breathin' at all!"

"He probably won't be soon, if he isn't taken off and looked after. . . . Then you'll have another death on your conscience."

"I ain't got no conscience," Macey said.

Rosie began to snivel again.

"All you need to do is call up on the RT," Lowe persisted. He was looking at Baker, not at Macey. "The weather's still good. He'd be off in an hour or two. It might save his life."

"An' I'd be off too," Macey said. "You can't pull that one, kid.

I told you before, I'm stayin' here. . . . So Chris'll just 'ave to stay too."

Baker was restive. "I reckon he will die, King. . . . He looks terrible."

"So what . . .? He brought it on himself, didn't he? I bet he *was* goin' to bust that light."

"Maybe be he was," Baker said, "but that don't mean we can just let him die."

"I ain't gain' to jack it all in now for Chris or anyone," Macey said.

"We're his mates, King . . ."

"Can't help that—he'll just 'ave to take his chance. Like in a war."

"But it ain't a war," Rosie said.

"It's my war, baby. . . . You want 'em to top me?"

Rosie was silent. They were all silent. Macey toyed ostentatiously with his gun.

"So now we can all stop bunnyin'," he said after a moment, "an' get a bit o' discipline back in the place. . . . Which reminds me, what 'appened to Chris's knife. Tommy?"

"Reckon it's still up there," Baker said.

"Better get it. An' keep it on you."

"I don't need it, King. . . . I don't want it."

"I said get it!"

Baker got slowly to his feet.

"An' while you're up there," Macey said, "clean that floor up, see. . . . Take a pail. . . . Stairs, too. . . . When you done that, we'll put the ropes back on these geezers. Don't want any more trouble. . . ."

The night was grim—and not only because of the murder. Mitchell, at least, was dead and gone. Robeson and Lowe could inwardly mourn, could inwardly rage, but he was no longer a problem to them or anyone. Hines still was. Not that the keepers cared about his ultimate fate—but wilful neglect of any sick man was hard to take. Also, Hines was disturbing. Around eleven in the evening he began to snore in a deep, unnatural way. The reverberations, penetrating the living-room, made it difficult for the keepers to get any rest—and impossible for Baker and Rosie to forget, even for a moment, that Hines was being callously abandoned. Even when, in the early hours of the morning, the snoring died down, the tension in the living-room remained. Baker was going through the motions of keeping watch during alternate hours, but at three Macey caught him dozing when he was supposed to be awake and after that he didn't dare to relax himself. The eyes of the keepers were rarely closed for long, he noticed—and now they had something to avenge. He felt less inclined than ever to put his trust solely in the ropes.

It was a relief for all when morning came—but especially for Macey. Now, he thought, as Lowe was dispatched to switch off the light and generator, perhaps they could forget about the previous day's upset and get back to a smooth routine. He gave brisk orders for breakfast when Lowe returned, and then went up to the gallery for his usual morning stroll, taking Robeson with him at gunpoint. He stood leaning over the rail, well away from the keeper, filling his lungs with the pure air and gloating over the tower below him. It was still his tower, still his moated castle. There'd been a bit of passing trouble inside it, that was. . . . Yet the morning promenade somehow lacked its customary zest. Macey hadn't thought of it before, but the fact was that the death of Mitchell and the injury to Hines had diminished his kingdom. . . .

His feelings of discontent grew sharper as the day advanced. He'd said he was going to restore discipline to the lighthouse, but instead it appeared to be breaking down completely. It wasn't that Baker or Rosie disobeyed any orders—he'd have known how to deal with that. It was just that for much of the time they weren't around when they were wanted. Their chief concern now seemed to be with Chris. They kept slipping away to look at him, which was stupid considering the state he was in. After a short period of delirium, during which he'd babbled horribly, he'd grown quieter and quieter and was now lying in total unconsciousness, with a waxy face, scarcely seeming to breathe.

Macey wished he'd die if he was going to, and get it over with. It was plain that nothing could be done for him, or about him. . . . But Tommy and Rosie just wouldn't see it that way. They were going around looking anxious all the time. Every glance they gave Macey seemed to reproach him for not calling up help on the telephone. They'd listened almost disbelievingiy when Robeson had been allowed to make only his standard call to the land that morning. . . . Soft, that's what they were. . . . Sentimental kids. . . . Not fit to have a leader like Macey. All the same, it was better to have them around than to have no one. You'd got to have one or two followers to give orders to. There wouldn't be much kick in being a commander if you'd no one to command except a couple of prisoners. . . .

Macey's thoughts switched to the keepers. That was another trouble. Robeson and Lowe weren't bothering to do their job properly any more, either. They'd polished the optic and washed the lantern and done what was necessary for the light, but that was all. They hadn't started to do any cleaning of the tower until Macey had made them. Lowe wouldn't have done any cooking if Macey hadn't poked the gun at him. Neither of them had shown any inclination to do anything. Except watch Macey. . . . Well, they'd better look out. . . .

At two o' clock that afternoon, Baker went down alone to the bottom of the tower. He'd seen from a window that the tide was low enough for a walk over the rocks, so this time he'd be able to get the air and exercise he needed. Also, he wanted to get right away from Macey, if only for a little while. He felt crushed by the weight of his disillusionment over Macey. He hadn't any doubt now that Macey had shot the cinema manager on purpose. He knew that he'd killed Mitchell without any good reason. And now there was Chris. . . . Baker couldn't get the thought of Chris out of his mind. Not that he'd ever liked him very much—it was Macey he'd followed. But that wasn't the point—you had to be loyal to your mates. Chris had been one of the gang, he'd been in on all the jobs—and Macey was going to let him die without lifting a finger. It was a rotten, lousy thing to do. Baker was sure now that Chris would die—and it was horrible to watch. . . . It made him so miserable that he almost wished he could die himself. . . .

He drew the entrance doors back and looked out. There was almost no wind and the sea was scarcely rippled. The air felt pleasantly cool on his face. He descended the gunmetal ladder to the set-off and walked slowly round the base of the tower. On the side where the rock fell sheer away, he paused. That would be where the keepers had given Mitchell his burial. Mitchell must be lying down there now. . . . Baker suddenly remembered what Rosie had told him about the kite-fishing. Mitchell had been quite a kind man, really. . . . He turned away sadly and walked round to the ladder and started to go down the last few rungs to the rocks.

He had taken only a couple of steps when, looking down, he saw something gleaming just below him in the pale sunlight. Something yellow. . . . He gazed at it in astonishment. It was the rubber dinghy that he'd left on the cruiser's cabin top. One of its rope handles was hooked over a metal rung, just below high water mark. It must have got caught up there after it had been washed off the top of the cruiser—and because of the set-off, it hadn't been visible from the tower.

Baker unhooked it, carefully, and carried it down to the rocks. It was partially deflated, but it didn't seem to be damaged at all. The inflator was still in the pocket provided for it, and the two small paddles were secure and intact. Screened under the tower's massive base, Baker inflated the dinghy. The air stayed in. It looked terribly tiny—but it was a boat. . . . Baker's eyes turned achingly to the distant shore. . . .

Rosie, too, had gone to an extremity of the tower to be out of Macey's way. Baker found her mooning alone in the lantern room.

"Hi Rosie. . . . Say, I got news for you."

"Bet it ain't good news," she said.

"I reckon it is. . . ." He paused, as voices reached them from below. "Come outside a minute."

She followed him out on to the gallery. "Well . . .?"

"That rubbber boat—the yellow one, remember? It's still there
. . ." He told her about hin find. "An' it's okay. It's all pumped up
an' it's got paddles an' everything."

She stared at him for a moment in silence. Then she looked over
the rail. "What you done with it?"

"Put it back the same place where I found it. It's safe—it won't
wash away. . . . Rosie, you an' me could try for a getaway in it."

Rosie gazed across the quiet sea to the faint outline of Sheep
Head. It's an awful long way, Tommy."

"Eight miles."

"You ever rowed eight miles?"

Baker shook his head, "Never 'ad to before. . . . Reckon I could,
though."

"It ain't much of a boat."

"It ain't too bad—not just for the two of us. It don't leaks any
rate. An' it can't sink, not with air in it."

"It could tip over."

"Not if we was careful. . . . Not while the sea's like this."

"I'd be scared, Tommy."

"I'm scared stayin' here," Baker said. "I reckon Chris was right,
Rosie—King's a nutter. I reckon he'll go on killin' till there ain't
no one left. . . . You want to stay here with King?"

Rosie shuddered. "I don't ever want to see him again. He ain't
what I thought, Tommy. He don't care what he does. He don't
care about me or anyone . . ."

"That's right," Baker said. "He ain't got no feelings. . . . You
goin' to come, then?"

"I dunno . . ." Fear fought against fear in Rosie's mind. "Maybe.
. . . When you thinking of going. Tommy?"

"Sooner the better, I reckon."

"To-day?"

"No, too late to-day—we'd get lost in the dark. Soon as it gets
light in the mornin' would be the best time. . . . What about it,
eh?"

Rosie hesitated.

"Think I'll take a chance, Rosie, any rate. . . . While the weather's okay."

"On your own, you mean?"

"If I 'ave to . . ."

Rosie looked down at the sea again. It *was* pretty smooth. . . .

"All right," she said, "I'll come . . . I ain't goin' to be left alone with him."

There was little the conspirators could do by way of preparation—but what they could do, they did. Food, water and warm clothes, Baker said, were what they'd need to take. They had their chance to hide a few things away at five that afternoon, when Macey was standing over Robeson at the RT and Lowe was up on the gallery. Baker quickly stuffed the pockets of his leather jacket with food from the living-room pantry. Rosie found an old vinegar bottle in a cupboard and filled it with water at the sink. Then Baker took the jacket and the bottle and Rosie's outdoor clothes down to the store room and hid them behind the paint tins. They could pick them up there in the morning on their way out. A little later, when Macey was listening to the news on the radio, Baker managed to extract a couple of thick blue jerseys from one of the lockers in the bedroom, and add them to the things in the store room. Now everything was set. . . .

It was difficult, through the long evening and the night, to behave naturally, to show no excitement, Rosie solved the problem by saying she was tired and pretending to doze off in one of the chairs as soon as the keepers were roped. She'd already refused to sleep in the bedroom where Hines was lying. . . . Baker took refuge in a stolid silence. His chief anxiety was about the weather. With one short interval, the sea had been calm now for five days. It couldn't stay like that much longer. But there was no sound of wind against the panes. They were all right so far. . . .

With the room lights kept on, as Macey insisted they had to be for safety, sleep was little more than a succession of uneasy snatches for anyone. By seven in the morning, Rosie was fully awake. As daylight showed at the window, Baker gave her a little nod, signalling that the time had come. Rosie got up and stretched and moved towards the door.

Macey said, "Where you goin'?"

"Where d'you think ...? Ain't much privacy here, I must say." With a toss of her head, Rosie went out.

Baker waited. It wasn't his hour for keeping an eye on the roped men, so he was free to move around—but he didn't want to seem in a hurry. Presently he got up, walked to the window in a leisurely way, looked out, and walked back again. He gave a huge yawn—a yawn of tension, not of tiredness. "Think I'll go an' take a gander at Chris," he said, Macey grunted.

Baker went out, and quickly descended the stairs. For the moment, he felt safe—Macey wouldn't leave the keepers on their own. He found Rosie in the store room, putting on one of the jerseys under her coat. She was shivering with excitement. "I'm scared, Tommy," she said. "Honest, I'm so scared. . . ."

"We'll be all right," Baker said—though he felt cold with fear himself. He put on the second jersey, pushed the water bottie into a pocket, and zipped up his leather jacket, "Okay—let's go."

They crept down to the entrance door and let themselves out. They couldn't close it behind them, but once they were away it wouldn't matter. The air was sharp, but the morning promised to be bright. In the east, there was already a hint of sun. Baker went ahead down the ladder to the set-off, calling to Rosie to take her time and not look down. He'd forgotten about the vertical ladder until now. He watched her, encouraging her, wondering if she'd be able to manage it. But Rosie made no fuss. In any other circumstances she would hardly have dared to risk it, but she was too concerned about Macey's gun behind and the sea in front to worry about falling. She threw her torn shoes down and descended in stockinged feet and in a few moments she was safely beside Baker. From the set-off she watched him collect the rubber boat on his way to the rocks. Then she joined him there.

The tide was fairly high, and rising. Much of the reef was already covered, but there was still a small dry platform of rock at the base of the tower, falling away sharply into deep water at its edges. The sea looked quiet enough away from the reef but around the rock the slight well was breaking constantly in spray. Getting into the dinghy, Baker saw, wasn't going to be easy. It would have to be done directly from the rock because the water around was too deep for wading. . . . He tried launching the boat and holding it close to the lee side of the reef while Rosie climbed in, but he couldn't hold it steady enough. The first time, a wave carried it over the rock just as she stepped in, so that when she sat down it wasn't floating. At the second attempt she almost went headlong into the sea. She looked in dismay at the bobbing craft. "Don't see how we'll ever get in," she wailed. "It ain't a proper boat at all. . . ."

Baker sat back on his heels, frowning. "Reckon we better just sit in it," he said, "an' wait for the tide to take us off."

He found a flat, weed-covered surface at the water's edge and placed the dinghy carefully and helped Rosie in. Then he got in too. They sat facing each other on the thin rubber bottom, arms resting on the inflated sides.

Baker looked up at the tower. The light of the optic was very faint in the brightening day. Suddenly it went out. Somebody was on the move. Probably Macey had freed Lowe and taken him up to the lantern. Next thing, they'd both be out on the gallery. And where the dinghy was now, it would be visible from the gallery. . . . Baker waited tensely. They weren't safe yet from Macey's gun.

It seemed ages before the water rose high enough to float the dinghy, and by then they were both soaked with spray. When the little boat did lift, its first movement was higher on to the rock. But now they were ready for the surge. As a wave approached they both leaned out, pressing down on the rock, holding the boat where it was. When the wave receded they pushed hard and were carried off on the ebb. Baker seized the paddles and began paddling furiously. For a moment or two they seemed to hang at the edge of the rock, neither floating nor stranded. Then they were away. . . .

Baker smiled at Rosie. "Made a start, any rate," he said.

It took him a little time to get used to the technique of the paddies. Though one end of the buoyant craft was pointed and the other blunt, the boat seemed to move as easily backwards or sideways as forwards and the slightest unevenness of stroke sent it spinning in a circle. But skill began to come with practice and in a few minutes he was maintaining fair control.

"Well, we ain't going to get shot, that's one thing," Rosie said, pointing to the lighthouse.

Baker glanced back. "No, we're okay now." They were already well out of range of the tower.

"Goin' fast, ain't we?"

Baker nodded. "Reckon it's the tide takin' us, Rosie...."

Rosie digested that. "Where d'you think we'll finish up, then?"

"Can't really tell," Baker said. "Anywhere on the shore'll do me—I ain't fussy ..." He was paddling in the general direction of the distant land. At least there was no difficulty about deciding what to aim for.

They weren't at all comfortable in the boat. The thin rubber sagged so much under them that they felt they could easily go through the bottom. Water slopped around them, making them even wetter than they were already. There was no danger from it, because of the buoyancy, but it was very unpleasant.

Rosie said, "My feet ain't half cold."

"I'm pretty warm," Baker said. He stopped paddling and stripped off his leather jacket. "Like to put this round 'em?"

"Thanks ..." Rosie took it gratefully. "You're a nice boy, Tommy. You're kind."

Baker grinned, and paddled on. He felt fairly cheerful, in spite of the discomfort. The main thing, he told himself, was that the sea was quiet. There was a long, gentle swell that kept the dinghy constantly in motion, but the surface of the water was smooth and only the odd splash was coming over the side.

By now, they seemed to have the world entirely to themselves—a vast green waste, featureless except for an occasional patch of weed or other flotsam. There were no ships anywhere near and the lighthouse looked at least a mile away. The dinghy, Baker realised, was drifting farther away from Salmouth all the time. Sheep Head was a good deal fainter than it had been to start with. The land opposite them didn't seem to be getting much nearer, either. Still, they must be making some progress. . . .?

"Like a bite o' grub?" Baker asked presently.

Rosie shook her head. "I ain't hungry . . . I think I'm going to be sick." She looked very pale. In a little while she *was* sick.

"You'll be better now," Baker said hopefully. "You like to paddle for a bit?"

"Not if you ain't tired."

"No, I ain't tired. . . . Nice to be doin' something."

"What we going to do when we get to the land, Tommy?"

Baker made a face. "Got to get there first."

"I ain't half sorry for them keepers, stuck there with King."

Baker nodded.

"Not bad fellers, was they?"

"Not bad," Baker said.

There was a long silence now. Baker found he needed all his breath to keep up the rhythmic paddling. Rosie lay back against the inflated bow of the boat, her eyes closed. She was looking very pale again. . . .

It was about ten o'clock when Baker noticed that the outline of the lighthouse was growing sharper. He watched the tower for a while. Yes, it was definitely coming nearer. The tide must have turned. . . .

Rosie opened her eyes, looked around, and shivered.

"Still cold?" Baker said.

"Frozen."

"You better paddle, Rosie."

"All right—I'll try. . . . Think we can change places?"

"Yeah—if we're careful."

They squeezed past each other on hands and knees. Rosie took the paddles. "Mind you don't drop 'em," Baker said. She began to paddle. She was worse at it than Baker had been and it took her longer to get the idea, to keep the dinghy from rotating. But she stuck at it. A little colour was coming back into her face.

"Reckon we'll have to take turns to keep warm," Baker said. He took the packet of food from his coat pocket and ate some bread and cheese and chocolate. "Sure you don't want none?"

"Not while I'm paddling . . ." Rosie was gazing across the water with a worried expression on her face. "Tommy, I think we're getting nearer the lighthouse again."

"I know. . . . Tide's takin' us back."

"Then we ain't getting nowhere," Rosie said aghast.

"Yeah, we are. . . . You can see—we're between the lighthouse an' the shore now."

"We ain't far on our way, though."

"'Bout a mile, I reckon." Baker forced a smile. "Only seven more to do."

"We won't never do it," Rosie said.

"'Course we will. . . . We got to, Rosie. We just gotta stick at it. . . ."

Rosie went on paddling.

At about that time, Macey and Lowe were leaning over the rail of the lighthouse gallery, scanning the sea. Lowe had the binoculars and was studying the water immediately around the tower.

It had been nearly eight o'clock that morning before Macey had realised that something was wrong. Soon after seven he'd called for Baker to come and untie Lowe, so that the keeper could switch off the light and start getting breakfast. When Baker hadn't come, he'd shouted angrily up and down the staircase. He'd shouted for Rosie, too. In the end, he'd had to release Lowe without assistance, holding the gun well out of reach of a snatch. Then, with Lowe ahead of him, he'd gone in search of the errant pair. He'd started at the top of the tower and worked downwards. It hadn't taken long, because there was really nowhere much to search. When he'd come to the entrance doors, he'd found them open. And the set-off and rocks had been empty . . .!

He'd gone over the whole tower again then. He'd looked in every cupboard, every possible space. Lowe, in some agitation, had helped him. In the end, only one conclusion had been possible.

Baker and Rosie had walked out on the rocks and, either deliberately or by accident, had drowned. . .

Now Lowe was examining the surface of the water through the binoculars to see if he could find any trace of the bodies. He was doing it because Macey had told him to. He thought it was very unlikely that they'd still be around, unless they'd got caught up in some rock—by now the tide would have carried them far away. . . . He raised the glasses, pointing them at distant water, sweeping the horizon. Suddenly, with a sharp exclamation, he focused on an object. A yellow speck, with two darker specks. . . .

"Good lord!" he said softly. . . .

"What's up?"

"They're all right . . .! They're out there in a boat."

"Don't be ruddy daft," Macey said. "Where'd they get a boat?"

"Look for yourself . . ." Lowe passed the binoculars.

Macey took them. "Stand back, kid . . ." He motioned Lowe to the other side of the gallery. Even in a crisis, he was still careful.

With half his attention on Lowe, it took him some time to find the speck. Then, for a moment, he had it in focus.

"Blimey," he said, "you're right . . .!" He stared at Lowe. "It's the rubber boat what floated off the cruiser. . . . How'd they get that?"

"I've no idea . . ." Lowe looked up at the sky, then back at the sea. His face was grave.

Macey suddenly lost all control of himself, "Rotten bloody traitors!" he yelled, shaking his fist over the rail. "Left me in the bloody lurch. . . . Goin' to grass on me, they are. . . . Cor, if only I could get my hands on 'em . . .! Goin' to the bloody cops. . . ."

"I don't think you've much to worry about," Lowe said. "I wish you had."

"What d'you mean?"

"Unless some ship sees them, they'll never make it. . . . There's bad weather coming."

"You sure?"

"The barometer's gone down. And this swell means there's wind on the way. . . . In that skimming dish, they won't have a chance."

"Reckon they'll drown?"

"They're practically bound to . . ."

Macey's face cleared. "Well, they've asked for it, ain't they . . .? Sneakin' off like that. . . ." He examined the dinghy again. Even through the glasses, it was almost out of sight. "Ain't gettin' nowhere," he said with satisfaction. "Just goin' where they're took. . . ."

"You could have them picked up," Lowe said. "A call on the RT would do it."

Macey shook his head. "We been over that before, feller."

"What difference would it make to you . . .? In three weeks the relief boat will come, and then everyone will know you're here anyway. . . . Are you going to let those two kids drown for the sake of three weeks?"

"It ain't that."

Lowe looked at him disbelievingly. "You mean you *want* them to drown . . .? I thought Rosie was your girl friend."

"Bloody little bitch," Macey said. "Drowning's too good for 'er. . . ."

The atmosphere at breakfast was more charged than ever. Neither of the keepers did more than toy with his food. Macey stoked himself without enjoyment, sitting a little apart from the others and watching them all the time. Robeson had added his own fruitless appeal to Lowe's when he'd been told about the escape, and had now relapsed into a grim and dangerous silence. He was thinking hard about the new situation in the tower. Lowe's face was set. It seemed there were no limit to Macey's inhumanity. Hines, Mitchell, Rosie, Baker—friend or enemy, it was all the same. Nothing mattered but Macey. Appeal and argument were equally useless. The man simply wasn't accessible. . . . And now events were moving with terrifying speed. Lowe had the deepest forebodings about what was to come.

The tension eased slightly after breakfast, when the keepers went up to do their cleaning. With one of them up on the platform polishing the optic, and the other perched high on the ladder washing the panes, Macey could afford to disregard them for a bit. He leaned over the rail, gazing out to where the yellow speck had been. There was no sign of it any more. No sign of anything. . . .

Gloom settled on his face, and he turned away. His gloating satisfaction over the likely fate of the deserters had been short-lived. He was aware now of a creeping loneliness. Baker and Rosie hadn't been exactly cheerful company since Mitchell's death, but they'd been better than nothing. He'd never been on his own like this before, not as long as he could remember. He'd always had some gang to look up to him, to admire him, to give him strength. Now he was alone. His status as a leader had gone, because he'd no one to lead. His little kingdom had fallen to pieces. Only a few days ago, he thought bitterly, he'd had six people to do his bidding. Three henchmen and three slaves. Now, out of the six, only two remained. Two enemies, out to get him. . . . You couldn't count Chris. Chris was going to die. . . .

For a while, self-pity consumed him. He'd been let down by everyone. . . . If Chris hadn't taken things into his own hands, Mitchell wouldn't have been shot and Baker and Rosie wouldn't have gone off. . . . They'd none of them been any good—none of them had been worth the trouble he'd taken over them. A lousy lot, not worth bothering about. . . . All the same, he missed them. . . .

Then his mood changed. His circle of influence might have shrunk for the moment—but pretty soon he'd have a much wider audience. He'd been let down—but he wasn't finished. Anyone who thought that was making a big mistake. *He* wasn't going to die—not yet, anyway. And certainly not without taking a lot of people with him. He still had his gun—and the gun was as potent as ever. He could still frighten Lowe, and stop Robeson in his tracks, just by pointing it. They'd seen what a bullet had done to Mitchell—they wouldn't want it to happen to them. He could still force Lowe to fetch and carry and cook, and Robeson to report harmlessly on the RT at the proper time, postponing the show-down. He could still safeguard himself by taking one of the keepers around with him whenever he moved about the tower. He was still in full control. . . .

It wasn't until he started, late in the afternoon, to think about the arrangements he'd need to make for the night, that Macey came to realise just how dangerously the balance of numbers had turned against him in the tower.

The trouble was that he couldn't rope both the keepers up at the same time any more. He could force one of them to rope the other—and, to lessen the strain on him, that was what he'd done during the afternoon. Robeson had been roped for hours. But that still left one man free. Macey himself couldn't do any tying, because knotting ropes was a two-handed job and he'd have to lay the gun down. He'd have to put himself, unarmed, within reach of a muscular adversary. He couldn't risk that. Anything might happen. . . .

So, all through the coming night, either Robeson or Lowe was going to be free. That wouldn't matter as long as Macey kept awake and alert—as long as he didn't doze. But, in the end, he'd be bound to doze—if not the first night, the second. . . . And then the man who was free would get the gun. . . .

The alternative was to retreat to some place of his own, to barricade himself in, and leave the keepers to their own devices for the night. But that had great dangers, too. They would be able to talk, to plot, without risk of interference. The free man would be able to release the other. They would be able to roam the tower at will. And in the morning he wouldn't know *where* they were. . . . Of course, he'd still have his gun—but would that be enough? Against one, yes—but against two . . .? Suppose they laid an ambush for him?

It was an alarming thought. They could conceal themselves behind a door, or round the twist of the spiral. They might come at him without warning from two directions at once. It would still be dangerous for them—but by now they must both be desperate men. Robeson especially—he looked ready to risk anything. Robeson had changed since Mitchell's death. He'd seemed pretty easy-going before that—he'd been concerned mostly with the light. Now he looked hard, determined. . . . They might already be preparing for a concerted rush. It could easily happen. In fact it was almost bound to happen some time, now that they were two against one.

There would be no more security in the tower, while they were two against one. . . .

Two against one. . . .

Well, there was a simple way out of that!

Macey sat with the gun in his lap, coldly pondering the most convenient method. He didn't expect any trouble from the second man, but it might be safer not to have him around at the time. And there was no point in making a bloody shambles of the tower again. . . . Or wasting a bullet. . . .

Presently, he stirred. "What about a cuppa, kid?"

Lowe filled the kettle and put it on the stove. The fire needed attention and he made it up.

"Better fetch some more coal," Macey said.

In silence, Lowe picked up the scuttle and left the room.

Macey walked to the window. The tide was low. "Reckon I'll take a stroll on the rocks," he said. "You'd better come too, Daddy-O—do you good." He undid Robeson's ropes. He could do that safely with one hand. "Okay—down you go . . ."

Robeson went ahead. After his cramped afternoon he was glad to be able to stretch his legs. They passed the winch room, where Lowe was still filling the scuttle, and descended to the entrance room. Robeson unbarred the door and looked out. A breeze had got up from the south and the sea was no longer placid. The sun was going down in a stormy sky.

"You first," Macey said, pointing to the ladder. Robeson swung himself on to it with practised ease and started to descend. There was a moment when he was holding the top rung with both hands. Macey stepped forward and ground his heel into the hands, one after the other. Robeson gave a shout of pain. His fingers loosed their grip. Macey helped him on his way with a vicious shove from his foot. Robeson lurched back, tried to grab the ladder again, failed, and fell with a crash to the stone set-off twenty-five feet below.

At Macey looked down, his worries over, Lowe appeared. "What was that noise? What's happended?"

Macey turned the gun on him. "Looks like it's just you an' me now, kid."

White-faced, Lowe gazed down. Robeson was a crumpled, motionless heap on the stone.

"Slipped off the ladder," Macey said. "Poor geezer's broken 'is neck."

Lowe turned on him wildly. "You pushed him. . . . You've killed him . . ." He started towards the ladder.

Macey stuck the gun in him. "You can cry over 'im later, kid—I need that cuppa. . . . Up you go . . .! An' just keep a civil tongue, will you. . . ." He was feeling quite cheerful again. Now it was one against one. . . .

Chapter Six

Lowe hardly knew how he reached the top of the tower. His head was reeling, his legs felt like putty. On the stairs, he had to cling to the iron handrail for support. Only the thrust of Macey's gun behind him drove him on. For the moment he was beyond all thought. A single stark emotion crowded out all else. *Horror.* . . . A paralysing horror of the monster at his back. . . .

In the living-room he waited, motionless, for Macey to speak.

Macey said, "Well, don't just stand there. . . . Char ain't goin' to get itself."

Mechanically, Lowe made the tea and poured it out. Macey said, "Let's have a bit o' cake, eh?" Lowe got that too. Then he sat down, holding his head, averting his eyes. He couldn't bear to watch Macey, swilling tea and munching cherry cake as though he'd just come in from a healthy country walk.

Presently he said, "I must get some air, Macey. . . . Can I go up on the gallery?"

Macey finished his cake and drained his mug. "Sure. . . . Reckon I'll come with you. . . ." His thin mouth twisted. "If you ain't got no objection, that is."

Lowe looked at him with loathing.

"You better start gettin' to like me, kid," Macey said. "We goin' to be alone together for a long while."

Lowe went out, swaying a little, and climbed blindly up the stairs. Macey followed close behind him—though not too close. Out on the gallery he took up a position a couple of yards or so away from Lowe. He began to whistle in an unconcerned way.

Lowe drew deep breaths of the salty air, turning his face to the wind. It was better out on the gallery. Slowly, his giddiness and nausea passed, leaving him cold with sweat.

He looked down in hopeless misery at Robeson's body, sprawled on the set-off. He'd been shocked at Mitchell's murder—but for Robeson he felt real grief. He'd had a deep affection for the old man, an enormous respect. It seemed incredible that a creature like Macey should have been able to destroy him. Yet there he lay, finished.... There'd be no more counsel from him, no more guidance, no more kindly words. Lowe was on his own....

He gazed out at the darkening water. Big seas, tipped with white, were beginning to rail in from the south-west. He thought of Macey's other victims, Baker and Rosie, still tossing out there, still drifting to and fro on the tide. He'd been right about them—they hadn't a chance. He knew just what would happen—if it hadn't happened already. At some moment, a breaking crest would topple their tiny boat and fling them into the sea. A moment of terror—and that would be the end.... He almost envied them. They, at least, had escaped this inhuman devil in the tower. They'd missed the dreadful final acts—the last of which, Lowe felt, would surely involve himself. After so much casual violence, it would be a miracle if he survived. Robeson had been killed because Macey thought him a danger—there couldn't be any other reason. And in the end, the same motive would apply to him. Macey might say they were going to be together for a long while, but once he had to face an outside enemy he would hardly want one at his back as well....

For a while, Lowe was close to despair. There seemed nothing he could do to change the course of events. Mitchell had been an impetuous man of action, and Macey had killed him. Robeson had been wise and cautious, and Macey had killed him. Where better men had failed, Lowe thought, what chance was there for him? He felt desperately unequal to the situation. Unequal to the responsibility....

Then, as he looked down again at Robeson, his mood changed. A wave of anger swept over him at the wicked, wanton crime. Of anger—and with it, the beginnings of resolve.... Who, after all, was Macey, that anyone should cringe to him? A crude and stupid gangster, with a gun. . . . Without the gun, he'd be nothing. Lowe would have seized eagerly, confidently, any chance to grapple with him as man to man. It wasn't Macey's strength that he feared—only his gun. . . . Perhaps he feared it too much. What, he asked himself, had he to lose? Hardly more than Macey himself. Life—sweet life. . . . But one could cling too hard to life, perhaps. . . . He thought of his father, who over and over again had risked his life in raging seas, knowing the risk, knowing just what he was doing. . . . And anyhow, Lowe thought, if at some point he was likely to be shot whatever he did, he might just as well try and make a fight of it. . . .

But how? What could he do? A fight was one thing—suicide was another. If he was to fight, it must be with judgment, with good timing. Nothing would be gained by flinging his life away. To try and grab the gun while Macey was alert would be precisely that. He must make his moment—or seize his moment. . . . And the time might come. How long, he wondered, could a man in Macey's position remain alert? His thoughts turned, as Macey's had, to the night ahead. To the obvious fact that Macey couldn't tie him up, without risking a struggle on equal terms. To the certainty that at some time he must sleep. That would be the moment to watch for, to wait for. . . . There might, after all, be a chance. . . .

Lowe felt a little better now. The inward communing, the tacit acceptance of responsibility, had strengthened him. He couldn't bring back Mitchell, or Robeson, or Baker, or Rosie—but he might still save himself. Anyway, he would do what he could. . . .

He looked again over the sea. Dusk was near. He turned and went into the lantern room, slowly, quietly, not asking permission, forcing himself not to glance at the gun. He heard Macey following him—without protest.

At the bedroom, Lowe looked in on Hines. Macey waited outside. Hines's coma had deepened, his breathing now was so shallow as to be barely perceptible. His face was parchment-white under its dark stubble of beard. He looked as though at any moment he might slip away. Well, there was nothing to be done for him. . . .

Lowe went down to the engine room and switched on the

generator. Then he returned to the lantern and switched on the light. Whatever happened, that was a routine that would have to go on till the end. . . .

The evening was hard to bear. Lowe longed to get away from Macey, to go to some room where be could sit alone and think and plan, but his presence seemed to be required. Macey obviously felt the need for company. He had become more talkative since supper—revoltingly so. All the things he talked about were aimed at the aggrandisement of Macey. The foolish indiscipline of Hines, which had brought its own penalty. . . . The stupidity of Rosie and Baker, choosing to drown rather than stay with him. . . . The jobs he'd done, the hold-ups he'd organised, the wads of money he'd collected for a few minutes' effort. . . . The fact that he still had more than twenty rounds of ammunition in his pocket, and was prepared to use them all. . . . Lowe replied to direct questions in monosyllables, volunteering nothing—just listening and watching. No more seemed to be demanded of him. All Macey needed was an audience for his malice and his boasting—and someone, from time to time, to do his bidding. He kept finding small jobs for Lowe. The fire needed stoking, the kettle refilling, the water pumping. . . . Once, in the arrogance of his upstart authority, he even asked Lowe to look at the tell-tale and make sure the light was working. . . .

Lowe carried out all instructions with convincing resentment, but without open hostility or demur. He knew that Macey already felt contempt for him and he played his part accordingly. To give the impression of forced compliance, of craven acquiescence, made obvious sense if he was ever to catch Macey off his guard. Hopes for the coming night sustained him. . . .

They were short-lived. A little before ten o'clock, Macey got up and stretched. "Reckon we better get some kip," he said. "Had quite a day, ain't we?" He eyed Lowe sardonically.

Lowe waited.

"Want to know the arrangements, kid?"

Lowe shrugged, "It doesn't make any difference to me."

"Makes a difference to me, though. . . . I'll tell you. . . . Go an' get a mattress from the bedroom an' shove it on the floor in the service room. . . . Two blankets an' a pillow, too. . . . I'm dossin' up there."

With a closed face, Lowe went and collected bedding from the bunk alongside Hines's, and carried it upstairs.

In a moment, Macey joined him. "Right, kid—that's all for now. See you bring me a cup o' char at eight o'clock in the mornin'. . . . You can fix yourself up how you like. 'Ave a nice rockabye . . .!" He pushed the door shut. Lowe heard the mattress being dragged across the floor and guessed what was happening. Macey would lie with his feet braced against the door, so that any pressure on it from outside would wake him instantly. And the gun would be ready to hand. . . .

In deep dejection, Lowe returned to the living-room. He could see now that he wasn't going to be given any chance—now or later. This way, Macey would get all the sleep he needed. This way, he would always be fresh and alert. In the morning he would be waiting with the gun, and the old round would start again. It would go on, day after day, till the final bloody reckoning. . . .

For a while Lowe sat silent, trying to think of some other plan. He had the run of the tower, now, but he couldn't see that it helped him. He had no light powerful enough to flash a signal—except the tower light itself, and to use that was unthinkable. In any case, it would only precipitate the end he feared, not avoid it. . . . What else . . ? A one-man ambush was out of the question. Wherever Macey went, the gun would precede him. . . . Lowe's imagination began to range more widely. What about morphia tablets in the morning tea?—there were some in the cupboard there, in the first-aid box. But Macey would know at once—the tea would taste like medicine. . . .What about some sort of booby trap. . .? A possibility—but hard to arrange, and fatal if it failed. . . .

He turned the radio on and stood listening to the weather forecast. A depression was approaching from the Atlantic. . . . Lowe needed no telling—the big swell and the sagging barometer were sufficient evidence. For the first time in days, he could hear the wind moaning through the lantern ventilators. The quiet spell had come to an end. . . .

He thought of Robeson's body on the set-off. If the weather got bad, the waves would batter it—perhaps without claiming it. He couldn't just leave it there. The old man would have wanted a decent burial—and a word spoken over him. A good man had the right to someone's tears. . . . Lowe took a torch from the cupboard and went down to the store room. The only piece of tarpaulin had been used for Mitchell, but there was still a pig of iron ballast that would weight the body. Lowe tucked it under his arm and threw a coil of rope over has shoulder and went down to the entrance door. He wouldn't be able to launch the body into deep water, unaided, but anything would be better than leaving it where it was. He opened the doors. The wind outside was gusty. Spray was driving over the set-off from the western end of the reef. Lowe shone his torch down on the huddled shape of the principal keeper—and gasped. . . . The shape had moved. Robeson was sitting up.

Lowe was down the ladder in seconds. "*Rob* . . .!" he cried.

The keeper was slumped back against the tower wall. His face was streaked with blood, his hair matted with brine, his clothes soaked. He looked as though the effort to sit up had exhausted his strength. But he was fully conscious, and lucid.

"Hallo, Jim," he said in a feeble voice. "Glad you've come, boy. . . ."

"I thought you were dead . . ." Lowe dropped down beside him. "You didn't move. . . . Macey said you were dead. . . ." He would never forgive himself for not having made sure.

"Macey trod on my hands. . . . Made me let go . . ."

Lowe shone the torch on the lacerated fingers. "God . . .!" They were in a shocking state—but that couldn't be the worst thing, after such a fall. . . . "Are you badly hurt, Rob?"

"Not too bad," Robeson said faintly. "Left ankle's broken . . ."

"Anything else?"

"Head's not so good—must have hit it.... Bruises everywhere. ... I was lucky, though.... Rail must have broken the fall ..."

Lowe nodded. "Right, don't talk any more.... I'll try and get you inside...."

He glanced at the ladder. With torn hands and a broken ankle, the old man wouldn't be able to do anything for himself. And, strong though he was, Lowe knew he couldn't carry the keeper on his back up those slippery, vertical rungs.

"I'll have to winch you up," he said. "I won't be long...." He climbed quickly to the winch room and opened the door that looked out over the entrance door and the ladder. With practised hands he attached a strong rope to the winch wire and lowered the end to the set-off. Then he went down again and tied the rope under Robeson's arms in a bowline.

"Now see if you can stand, Rob ..." Gently, anxiously, he raised the keeper on to his one good foot. "All right so far?"

"Yes," Robeson murmured.

Lowe bent, and lifted him, and carried him the few steps to the bottom of the ladder. "Think you can hold on while I get up there?"

Robeson drooped his arms over one of the rungs, supporting himself. "Yes ..."

"I'll haul you up carefully.... You'll be all right."

Robeson nodded. His face was ashen in the torchlight. "Go ahead, boy—it's the only way ..."

Lowe raced up the ladder and climbed to the winch room. It was bound to be hell for Robeson—the best they could do was get it over.... He turned the winch handle, slowly, until the wire took the strain. He could almost feel in his own chest the pain of the taut rope round the keeper's bruised body. He clenched his teeth and went on turning. Occasionally, when the rope went slack, he guessed Robeson was resting on a rung, and waited. From time to time he braked the winch and went to the opening to see what progress they were making. Nearly there, now.... Another few feet.... He looked down again.... Robeson was safe, sprawled over the threshhold of the door.

He descended quickly to the entrance room, "Okay, Rob ...?"

"Just about . . ." Sweat glistened on Robeson's forehead. He looked pretty well all in.

Lowe untied the bowline. For a moment, he stood in doubt. It seemed unlikely that even Macey would want to complete his unfinished job on Robeson, now that the keeper was totally immobilised—but with Macey you couldn't be sure. Better to keep the truth from him as long as possible. . . .

"I'm going to carry you up to the store room," Lowe said. "You'll be safe there. . . ."

Slowly, carefully, he raised Robeson to a standing position and got him on to his shoulder. The keeper was heavy, but manageable. Step by step, gripping the rail of the spiral with his free hand, pausing on each landing for breath, Lowe climbed the four flights to the store room. There, he lowered the old man on to some empty sacks behind the wall of paint tins.

Robeson sank down with a sigh. "Thanks, Jim . . ."

"I'll soon have you fixed up now," Lowe said, "I'll be back. . . ." He hurried out.

As he climbed to the living-quarters, he mentally listed the things he would need. Dry clothes. . . .Blankets and a pillow. . . . Disinfectant and bandages for the hands. . . . More bandages and some sort of splint for the ankle. . . . Liniment for the bruises. . . . Water. . . .

He felt thankful, now, that Macey had retired to the service room. No sound came from the top of the tower. And all that he needed, he could get from the living-room and the bedroom. Busily, he collected the things together, made his orderly preparations. It was a relief to have something to do, a gratification to be tending someone after all the violence, to be assuaging pain. . . . And wonderful to know that Robeson was alive after all. . . .

He had to make several journeys before he was satisfied that he'd done all he could. Robeson was in dry clothes again, his massive bruises anointed, his head plastered, his hands bandaged, his foot splinted after a fashion. He'd drunk a mug of hot, sweet tea and swallowed four aspirins. Lowe drew the blankets over him.

Almost before he'd closed the store room door, Robeson was sinking into an exhausted sleep.

Methodically, Lowe covered up the traces of the night's work—coiling up the hauling-line he'd used, winding up the winch wire, closing all the doors, collecting his torch. Then he returned to the living-room.

He felt more cheerful than he'd been for days. No doubt it was irrational, because basically the situation hadn't improved, Robeson, though alive, was certainly in no state to give any help against Macey—and, with a broken ankle, wasn't likely to be. All the same, Lowe's feeling of utter isolation in the tower had gone—and his morale had bounded. The survival and rescue of Robeson seemed a kind of augury. Until now, Macey had won every engagement. Now, in a sense, he'd lost one. . . . That nights, Lowe even managed to sleep a little himself.

He was up well before daylight. His only chance of attending to Robeson, he knew, was while Macey still slept. The wind was moaning on a deeper note but there was no other sound in the tower. He made tea on she stove and prepared a plate of Robeson's favourite cereal and carried the things on a tray down to the store room. Robeson was awake.

"Morning, Rob," Lowe said.

"Hallo, Jim."

"Did you get any sleep?"

"Quite a bit."

"Good. . . . How are you feeling now?"

"Oh, fair. . . . Very stiff. . . . Everything aches."

"I'm not surprised," Lowe said. "Let's have a look at you . . . He examined the keeper's injuries. Both Robeson's eyes were circled with purple-black rings; his cut head was tender; his body was a mass of bruises; his ankle was like a balloon. He really was quite a wreck. But as far as Lowe could judge, he hadn't suffered any permanent damage. All he needed now was rest. . . .

"Here's some tea," Lowe said. He helped the keeper into a sitting position. "Think you can hold the mug?"

"Just about ..." Robeson's hand-bandages left the ends of his fingers conveniently free. He took the mug and drank gratefully.

Lowe put the plate of cereal beside him. "I've some more things to get," he said. "I won't be long."

He went back up the tower and collected various supplies that Robeson would need during the day—a bottle of water, a little food, some pain-killing tablets from the first-aid box, the keeper's pipe and tobacco and matches.... There was still no sound from above. Quickly, he returned to the store room.

"Thought I'd better stock you up a bit," he said. "If Macey sticks as close to me to-day as he did yesterday, I probably shan't be able to get down again before to-night.... Will you be all right?"

"I'm sure I will."

"I can't think of any reason why he should want to come down here.... Anyway, I'll do my best to keep him away."

"You're a good lad, Jim."

"Wish I could do more," Lowe said. "It's the same old deadlock up there with Macey."

"Where is he now?"

"Asleep in the service room—barricaded in."

"Does he still keep you covered all the time?"

"Every waking minute...." Lowe attended to Robeson's personal requirements, and made him comfortable. "Well, I'd better get back now, Rob.... see you to-night."

Robeson nodded. "Be careful, Jim ..." He sank back on the bed of sacking and closed his eyes.

Dawn was breaking as Lowe left the sick man. He went down to the engine room and cut the generator. Then he climbed to the lantern, tip-toeing past the service room, and switched off the light. On his way past the bedroom he looked in on Hines. There seemed to be no change in his condition.

Back in the living-room, he turned the radio on at low volume to get the news. The weather forecast was just ending. The outlook was more depressions and high winds. Lowe started to prepare breakfast for himself. His mind was so occupied with old and new problems that he scarcely noticed when the news began. Then his attention was suddenly held. . . .

"Here is an item which has just come in," the announcer said. "A youth and a girl walked into Lincombe police station, South Devon, early this morning, and stated that they had been concerned in the recent hold-up at the Majestic Cinema, Salmouth, when the manager was shot dead. They gave their names as Thomas Baker and Rose Cleeve. It is understood that they were in an exhausted condition after spending seventeen hours at sea in an open boat. No further information is available at present . . ."

Lowe slapped his left palm with his fist in a gesture of unalloyed delight. So they'd made it!—against all the odds. And, whatever they'd done before, they'd deserved to. . . . With a smile of pleasure, he switched the radio off. Good for them . . .!

Then, as the implications of the news sank in, his face grew grave again. Baker and Rosie had given themselves up. Sensible kids . . .! But that meant they were ready to tell everything. By now, or very soon, the situation in the tower would be known to the authorities. . . .

So everything was changed. The days of isolation were over. Suddenly, unexpectedly, the last act of the drama was at hand. . . .

Macey came down just before nine o'clock. "You in there, kid?" he called, from outside the sitting-room door. Lowe answered him. Macey opened the door cautiously, pointing the gun at the gap, making sure Lowe was standing well back before he entered.

"Blimey, you been doin' a yourself all right, ain't you?" Macey said, surveying the used breakfast crockery. "What about that cup o' char you was goin' to bring me at eight?"

Lowe had forgotten all about it. "You seemed to be asleep," he said. "I didn't think you'd want me to wake you."

Macey grunted. "Aw, well, you can get me some coffee instead. . . . An' I'll have two eggs an' two rashers this mornin'. . . ." He went over to the window, humming. He seemed to be in good spirits after his unbroken night. . . . Then Lowe told him the news.

At first, Macey refused to believe it. The wind was gusting hard

127

against the tower and there was a big sea outside. It seemed impossible that the pair could have got ashore only a few hours before. But at nine o'clock the news bulletin was repeated and Macey was able to hear the item for himself, in substantially the same form.

Lowe was prepared for an angry outburst then—but it didn't come. Macey merely scowled. "So much for you, Mr. Know-all. . . . Couldn't make it, you said. Not a chance, you said . . ."

"It was the wind going round to the south that did it," Lowe said, "They must have been blown ashore before the sea got up."

"Bloody little rats. . . ." Macey spoke without venom, as though it was all past history that didn't matter any more. "They'll grass, o' course. . . . They'll tell about what's been goin' on here."

"Lowe nodded. "It won't be long now before a boat comes out."

"Well, it don't make no difference to me," Macey said. "Three weeks' time, or to-day, or to-morrow—What's the odds? Just brought things on quicker, that's all."

"What are you going to do about it?"

"You know what I'm goin' to do, kid—I told you already. . . . Hold out."

"You can't be serious."

"Bet your life I'm serious. . . . We goin' to shut ourselves in, just the way I said. Bar the ruddy door an' turn the place into a fortress."

"It's crazy," Lowe said. "You haven't a hope."

"That's what you said about them two squealers," Macey jeered. "Ain't much of a prophet, are you?"

"I'm sure when the boat comes they'll get in somehow."

"We'll flippin' well see, won't we?"

"Even if they didn't," Lowe said, "What would be the point? You couldn't hold out for ever."

"I reckon I could hold out for six months."

"What good would that do?"

"It'd keep me alive for six months, kid, that's what good it'd do . . .! An' give me a lot o' kicks, too. . . . Man, am I ready for them geezers! I tell you, I'll shoot any bastard what comes near." Macey took a handful of cartridges from his pocket and let them slide back through his fingers, one by one, lovingly. "You still don't know me proper, do you? I'm real tough, I am. I ain't afraid o' no one. I ain't afraid o' nothin'. . . ."

Lowe gazed at the brutal, insensitive face, that registered so little. It might well be true, he thought, that Macey was afraid of nothing. Nothing, at least, that was within the range of his knowledge and limited imagination. Not of a gun. Or a knife. Perhaps not even a noose. He must have faced up to all these things in his mind. That was what made him so deadly. . . .

"Wouldn't be surprised if we was still 'ere next Christmas," Macey said. "Still fightin' it out. . . . I tell you, kid, you an' me's goin' to enjoy ourselves. . . . Now, then, what about them rashers?"

The seascape was impressive when Macey took Lowe out on to the gallery half an hour later. The tumbling waves were more white than green, and round the reef itself they were breaking in huge curtains of foam and spray.

Macey looked down—and frowned. "Robeson's body's gone. . . . You get rid of it, kid?"

Lowe shook his head. He'd already observed that the swell had been over the set-off and was still rising level with it. "The sea must have swept it away," he said, in a suitably sombre voice.

"Ah . . ." Macey seemed satisfied. "Saved you a bit o' trouble, eh . . .?" He gripped the rail tightly as a gust of wind tore at him. "Rough, ain't it?"

"It is blowing a bit," Lowe said. He stood for a moment, watching the sea and listening to the wind. It was a sight and sound that usually exhilarated him—but not to-day. Presently, with Macey at his back, he turned and went into the lantern room to start his chores.

He'd just begun to polish the optic when the telephone rang. He looked at his watch. The routine call wasn't due to be made for another half-hour so it couldn't be anything to do with that. This was probably the start of the show-down.

Macey seemed to think so too. "Come an' listen in, kid," he said. "This is goin' to be good." He motioned Lowe to the stairs with his gun. Lowe went down. Macey followed him. In the service room, he took up a nonchalant posture on the corner of the RT table and lifted the receiver.

"Yeah?" he said, holding the phone away from his ear so that Lowe could hear.

"Who's that?" a curt voice asked.

"You're havin' the pleasure of speakin' to 'King' Macey."

There was a slight pause. Then another voice spoke—a softer, more deliberate one. "This is Superintendent Wilson, of the Salmouth police . . ."

"Hurray for you!" Macey said, winking at Lowe.

"Listen, Macey—we know all about the situation in the lighthouse. In case you haven't heard, young Baker got ashore in a rubber boat and he's given us a full report."

"I heard."

"Very well. . . . A tender will be coming out to take you off as soon as the weather improves."

"That's what you think," Macey said.

"Now look, Macey—be sensible. . . . You've had a good run—but it's over. You must see for yourself that the game's up. You can't get away, there's nothing more you can do—you might just as well come quietly. What's the point of prolonging the business?"

"I like it here," Macey said, "Suits me constitution."

"You won't do yourself a bit of good, you know. You can't win . . ." The voice went on, calmly, rationally, repeating the phrases and arguments that Lowe had used himself, that Robeson had used days ago without effect. "If you give up now, you'll save a lot of trouble and unpleasantness for everyone. We don't want any more bloodshed. Isn't it enough that you've killed two men already . . .?"

"They got in me way," Macey said. "An' I'll, do the same to any other geezer what gets in the way. . . . That's a warning, copper."

"Why take more lives, if it can't help you . . .?"

"You're wastin' your breath," Macey said.

There was a sigh, a pause. Then the voice said, "Can I speak to Keeper Robeson?"

"No, you can't. . . . No one ain't speakin' to anyone except me, see."

There was another short pause. "Well, you'd better think over what I've said, Macey . . ."

"I done that, feller."

The telephone clicked.

"Cor, he's rung off . . ." Macey put the receiver down. Then he looked at Lowe complacently. "Well, what you think o' that, kid . . .? On their ruddy knees, ain't they . . .? 'Please, Mr. Macey, do come along quiet an' give us no trouble . . .' An' that's just the start. Bet all the big shots'll be ringin' up soon. Beggin' me to make it easy for 'em. . . . Prob'ly have the Home Secretary on the line next. . . . What a giggle, eh?"

Lowe could think of nothing to say. After a moment he went back to the lantern room to continue his polishing. He'd found the tone of the conversation most depressing.

The morning brought no fresh developments. Lowe got on with his work. Macey stayed with him all the time, dropping an occasional gloating remark, saying they mustn't miss the one o'clock news, fiddling contentedly with his gun. Lowe prolonged his cleaning at the top of the tower so that Macey should be kept away from the rooms below as much as possible. When Macey did go down, Lowe went with him. Passing the store room door, he talked volubly to cover any sound from within. He still felt anxious about the consequences if Robeson were discovered—though not acutely, for Macey was now in a most amiable mood. Lowe decided be must try and keep things that way, and went to some pains to prepare a specially good dinner.

The news bulletin at one o'clock proved to be all that Macey had hoped for. The seizure of the Swirlstone led the items, and the background was covered in detail. The bulletin recalled the cinema hold-up and gave the names of the four concerned. It told of the stolen cruiser, the passage in the fog, the taking over of the tower, the shooting of Keeper Mitchell and the injury to Hines, and the escape of two of the gang in a boat. Macey, the leader, it said, was still holding the remaining two keepers at gunpoint The police had been in touch with him by radio-telephone that morning, demanding his surrender, but Macey had been defiant. They were now consulting with Trinity House officials and harbour authorities about the next step. At the moment, further action was being hampered by bad weather. So far, the Swirlstone light had continued to function normally, but shipping was being warned of the situation. . . .

Macey listened avidly. This was his meat and drink, and his appetite was insatiable. After the announcer had said, "Now here is the rest of the news . . . he'd switched off, he insisted on mulling over every detail of the bulletin, savouring his triumph again.

"Wish we could see the ruddy papers to-morrow," he said. "Bet they'll 'ave a lot more stuff. . . ."

Several times during the afternoon he returned to the radio, trying to pick up more reports. Lowe had been hoping for a chance to slip away and bring Robeson up-to-date with all that had happened, but Macey gave him no opportunity. There had to be. an audience at the set, a public. . . . But nothing fresh emerged. . . .

Then, around four o'clock, the sound of an aeroplane engine took them both hurrying to the gallery—though even in his excitement Macey .didn't forget to make Lowe go first. . . . It was a small plane—it looked to Lowe like a chartered one. There were several men in it, beside the pilot, and most of them, had cameras. As it circled, Macey took off his keeper's jacket and waved to them impudently. The plane continued to fiy around for several minutes, battling the stiff breeze. Then it turned back towards the coast.

"Reckon we'll be on the telly to-night," Macey said. "Ruddy shame ours ain't workin'. . . . Photographers, that's what they was. . . . See their cameras, kid? Reporters, too, I wouldn't be surprised. . . . Next thing, they'll be rannin' trips out 'ere. . . ."

The evening passed quietly—too quietly for Macey. The news bulletins added little to what had been said during the day, and by repetition had lost most of their impact. Macey sat for a while by the telephone, like a cat at a mouse-hole, hoping that someone would come through with a fresh appeal or maybe an offer of terms which he'd enjoy turning down—but to his chagrin, it remained silent. He thought of trying to ring someone up himself, but decided it might give an impression of weakness. He started boasting again to Lowe, his captive audience, but found it a poor substitute for action. Around ten, he suddenly announced that he was going to turn in, and went off to the service room for the night.

Lowe gave him half an hour to settle down. Then he heated some food and made a pot of tea and took it down to Robeson with a few magazines and newspapers. It must have seemed a long day, he thought, for the old man.

Robeson was leaning against the wall with a pillow at his back. His eyes were still ringed with purple but he looked fairly cheerful and was obviously glad to see Lowe. His ankle was a bit painful, he said, in reply to Lowe's inquiry, but otherwise he was getting on fine.

"What's been happening up there, Jim?" he asked, as he started to eat. "I thought I heard a plane circling this afternoon."

"You did," Lowe said—and told him all the news. About Baker and Rosie, and the telephone conversation with the police, and the radio reports, and Macey's determination to hold out as long as he could. Robeson listened in amazement.

"Well, you have had a day!" he said at last. He still looked as though he couldn't quite believe it.

"Imagine those two getting through . . .! I never thought they would, not for a moment. . . . So now the whole thing's out, eh . . .?"

"Everything."

Robeson sat frowning. His second thoughts were not very different from Lowe's.

Presently he said, "The weather seems better. Not so much wind, is there?"

"No—and the glass is steady."

"Then the tender will probably be out first thing in the morning."

"I should think so." Lowe started to prepare fresh bandages for Robeson's hands. "What do you think they'll do, Rob?"

Robeson was silent for a long time. Then, slowly, he shook his head. "I don't know," he said. "I just don't know . . ."

The night was peaceful. Lowe, following Macey's example, had spread his own mattress on the sitting-room floor, and managed to get a good night's sleep. He woke to a promisingly fine morning, with little wind and a moderate sea. He attended to Robeson, and remembered to take Macey his cup of tea. The news bulletin at breakfast was little more than a rehash of old facts. Afterwards, Lowe and Macey went up to the lantern for the usual chores. . . .

It was just after eleven when the tender came into sight. It approached quickly from the north, a vessel of two thousand tons with the strength of a tug, dipping and bucking in the choppy sea and throwing up a fine bow wave. Lowe watched it through the binoculars. Macey stood apart, gun in hand. He looked quite unworried.

The tender slowed as it reached the tower, turned into the tide, and let go its anchor in the customary spot some four hundred yards away. Men moved to the starboard davits and lowered one of the motor boats. In a few moments, it was away. Lowe counted nearly a dozen men in it.

It approached the reef cautiously. There was no question at all of a landing—the rocks were white with foam. Slowly, it circled the tower. The men in it were all looking up at the gallery, several through binoculars. A man standing in the bows had a loud hailer in his hand. Macey waved to him with his gun. The boat manœuvred closer and the man raised the loud hailer. "This is the police. Macey," he called. "We've come to take you off. Throw your gun into the sea, and let the keepers pass us a rope. . . . Do you hear?"

Macey motioned to Lowe. "Get our loud hailer . . ." Lowe fetched it from the lantern room. He was going to hand it to Macey, but Macey made him put it down before picking it up himself. "Just keep back, kid . . ."

With one eye on Lowe, Macey leaned over the rail and blew a raspberry through the loud hailer.

The motor boat continued to circle. Some of the men were

pointing—to the set-off, the windows, the gallery. The policeman had put his loud hailer down. Some discussion seemed to be going on. . . . Then the boat sheered away and rejoined the tender. For a while it lay alongside. Through the binoculars, Lowe could see men gesticulating from boat to ship. . . . More discussion. . . . Then the davits were manned again and the motor boat was hauled aboard.

"See, kid?" Macey said triumphantly. "There ain't a thing they can do."

Lowe saw only too well—and not just because the motor boat had been withdrawn without achieving anything. He'd been aware of the problem since Macey had first talked of holding out. Robeson, of course, had been aware of it, too. Since yesterday the police had had to face it. They'd shown they were conscious of it when they'd called Macey up on the RT. They would never have been so argumentative, so placatory, if they'd felt in control of the situation. They'd have acted . . . The plain truth was that they had no control whatever—and, if Macey's resolution held, they wouldn't have in any foreseeable time. . . . In any foreseeable circumstances. . . .

It was all a question of access. In ordinary winter weather, of the kind that was likely from now on, there was only one way of getting men into the tower from a boat and that was with the help of those inside—which would be denied. . . . If, by chance, another very calm spell came along, the motor boat might succeed in landing men directly on to the rock—but then what? Short of dynamiting the entrance door, they wouldn't be able to get into the tower—and anyone who tried to approach the entrance door by that vertical ladder would be an easy target for Macey's gun. No sane man would dream of attempting it. . . .

An approach by helicopter would be just as dangerous. Macey had been right about that, too. Putting a man on to a lighthouse gallery in anything but the best of weather was difficult enough even without opposition, Lowe had seen it done. In face of a gun, it would be suicidal. Macey would simply shoot the man as he swung down. . . .

Of course, Lowe thought, someone ashore might have a brilliant idea. They must be working on it pretty hard. But at the moment he couldn't imagine any plan that would succeed. The truth was that the Swirlstone tower had been built to be impregnable—and it *was* impregnable, against anything but major assault and bombardment. And who would bombard it?—extinguishing the light and damaging the structure, not to mention sacrificing the lives of two keepers in the process. Lowe felt sure that no such extreme methods would be used. Obviously the authorities would wait, hoping they could wear Macey down, hoping that he'd crack—and knowing that in the last resort, however long it took, they could starve him out....

It was a grim prospect....

Macey said, "Time to get dinner, kid."

With a nod, Lowe set off down the tower. At the bedroom, he stopped. He hadn't been in to look at Hines that day. With all his troubles, he couldn't forget that the man was there, as Macey seemed to. He went in, Macey waited by the door.

Hines showed no sign of life at all. Lowe touched his hand. It was cold. So was his face. When Lowe tried to lift an arm he found it rigid.

"He's dead, Macey."

Macey grunted. "Taken his time, ain't he ...? Okay, you better carry him down an' get rid of him."

Lowe looked at Macey—and quickly away again, A macabre thought had suddenly come into his mind. Perhaps this was his opportunity....

"I can't carry him by myself," he said.

"'Course you can.... Got him down 'ere by your-self, didn't you?"

"He's as stiff as a board, Macey.... You'll have to help me."

Macey came slowly into the room. "Well, cover 'im up, then."

With some difficulty, Lowe wrapped the body in a blanket. "What shall I do—take his feet and go first?"

"Okay ..."

Lowe stood by Hines's feet, trying to watch the gun without

seeming to. Macey moved to the head, Lowe sensed, rather than saw, his hesitation. It was obviously going to be a two-handed job. . . . For a second, it seemed as though he was going to put the gun in his pocket. . . .

Then, with a look of cunning, he stepped back. "You tryin' something on, kid?"

"What do you mean?"

"Aw, don't come that innocent stuff. . . . I wasn't born yesterday."

"I still don't know what you mean."

"Thought you'd start a bundle, didn't you . . .? Well, I ain't givin' you the chance. We'll just leave him till he's softened up, see. Then you can take him on your own. . . ."

There was more activity around the tower that afternoon. Another private aeroplane appeared, and a naval helicopter circled for half an hour. Several fishing boats came out from Salmouth to have a look, and a coastguard launch paid a brief visit.

There was no further attempt at communication by the tender, and the telephone remained silent. Lowe wasn't surprised, for there seemed little that anyone could usefully say. No effective verbal pressures could be brought to bear on a man as lost as Macey. Lowe wondered, too, if the authorities' silence was perhaps a calculated policy. Macey's swollen ego would merely be sustained by signs of outside interest, by reminders that he had the limelight on him. Silence might well be the best weapon against him. The fact that the news bulletin at six had almost nothing to say about the lighthouse seemed to confirm the notion. A tender had gone out to reconnoitre the position, the announcer said. Otherwise, the situation hadn't changed. . . .

Wearily, Lowe started to prepare supper. He still didn't see how the situation *could* change—not as a result of outside action, anyway. . . . He still couldn't think of a single effective step the authorities could take. They could easily put on a show of force, of course—but the objections to that were even greater than to radio publicity. A destroyer standing by would be much more likely to encourage Macey than to overawe him. . . . Lowe wished he knew what was going on ashore, what was being said and planned. Obviously, tremendous conferences must be taking place. High-powered brains must be at work on the problem. Every conceivable possibility would be explored.... Lowe wondered again if someone would come up with a novel and workable plan—some new technique of assault, some unexpected manœuvre.... That seemed the only hope....

He had a long talk about it with Robeson after Macey had gone to bed—but the discussion didn't lead anywhere. The principal keeper, like Lowe, could think of no practical way of forcing an entry against opposition. The visit left Lowe with a new anxiety, for Robeson's ankle wasn't progressing at all well. The broken bone clearly needed expert attention. If something wasn't done about it very soon, the old man might well be lame for the rest of his days....

Before he turned in, Lowe went up to the gallery. The tender, he saw, was still anchored in the same spot, its lights blazing. Lowe found considerable comfort in its presence. Even though it could do nothing, the mere fact that it was standing by was a great help to morale. Probably, he thought, that was the idea....

The shock was all the greater in the morning when, glancing out of the sitting-room window after he'd attended to Robeson, Lowe saw that the tender had gone. He went up to the lantern, thinking that some other vessel might have replaced it, but the tossing grey sea was empty. There wasn't a craft of any sort in sight. His spirits sank to a new low. He felt abandoned, deserted....

It wasn't until after dinner that day that he discovered why the tender had gone. He was in the sitting-room with Macey and had just turned on the radio to get the one-forty shipping forecast.

"First," the announcer said, "here is the general situation. An unusually deep depression is approaching from the south-west and intensifying. Winds of storm force or violent storm force are expected in many sea areas...."

At once, Lowe's attention was riveted. He listened carefully while the announcer went through the area reports.

"... Sole, Fastnet, Lundy and Plymouth. Wind west, backing to south-west, force 10, violent storm force, gusting to force 11 or perhaps hurricane force 12 Fair. Visibility poor."

Lowe glanced at Macey. If he had taken it in, he showed no sign. He was in a sulky mood because of the lack of news about himself.

"I'm just going up to the service room," Lowe said.

"What for?"

"To look at the barometer."

"Okay ..."

Lowe raced up the two flights. He could scarcely believe his eyes when he saw the glass. It had fallen more than an inch since breakfast—faster, and to a lower point, than he'd ever known it. He stood staring at it for a while. Then, with a thoughtful look on his face, he returned to the living-room.

"The glass has dropped like a stone," he said.

Macey grunted.

"I'll have to close the shutters, Macey."

"What shutters?"

"Over the windows."

Macey looked at him suspiciously. "What for?"

"We're in for a bad storm. If the windows aren't shuttered, the sea might smash them and come pouring in."

Macey stared at him. "What—up 'ere?"

"I'll say.... A big sea could sweep right over the tower—and there's enormous weight in water."

"Yeah ...?"

"You don't realise.... Do you know, a wave once tore a big bell from its bracket near the top of the Bishop lighthouse—a hundred feet above sea level."

"Well, it ain't like that now," Macey said.

"It's going to be."

"You're very sure o' yourself all of a sudden, kid."

"I'm only sure about my job," Lowe said. He went quietly to the door and switched on the electric light. Then he crossed the room and drew a pair of heavy gunmetal shutters over the window. Now only two small panes of plate-glass let in any daylight.

"Lot o' boloney, I reckon," Macey said, in a grumbling tone.

"You'll see. . . . I know what I'm doing." Lowe stood silent for a moment, wondering what he should do about the other windows—about Robeson's windows. . . . He'd have to close them—but Macey would want to come down with him, as likely as not. . . .

His glance fell on the kettle, simmering on the stove.

"Like some tea?" he asked.

"Sure," Macey said. "Never turn down a cup o' char."

Lowe warmed the pot and made the tea. He poured a steaming, brimming cup for Macey, and passed it to him. He cooled his own with milk, and drank it quickly. "I'd better do the rest of the shutters," he said—and slipped out.

He paused on the floor below to see if Macey was following him—but he wasn't. The trick had worked. Quickly, Lowe descended to the store room. Robeson was sitting up, reading a book that Lowe had brought him that morning.

"Hallo, Jim," he said in surprise. He hadn't had a daytime visit before. "Something the matter?"

"Only the weather . . ." Lowe went over to the window and closed the shutters.

"In for a dirty spell, are we?"

"The lot," Lowe said, "They're talking of force 12."

Robeson gave a low whistle. "Is the tender still around?"

"No, it's gone. . . . I'll have to get back, Rob. Anything I can do for you?"

"I'd like the light on, Jim, that's all."

Lowe pressed the switch. "I'll be seeing you, then . . ." He went out, closing the door behind him. No light showed through at the bottom. There was still no reason why Macey should go into the room. . . .

He went on down, checked that the entrance doors were properly secured, and worked his way up again, closing the shutters in every room, on every landing. Now they were battened down, and ready for anything. . . .

The wind got up quickly. At midday it had been only a whisper. By three o'clock it was blowing hard against the shutters and whistling through the ventilators like a train. As the afternoon wore on, a new sound was added to the noise—the thump of big sea beginning to break over the set-off. It was sound that Macey hadn't heard before, and it seemed to bother him a bit. Presently he found a radio programme he liked at turned the volume up to drown the noise. Lowe sat opposite him, an unread book on his knee, deeply preoccupied.

When the programme ended, Macey become restive. "Don't like it in 'ere with window covered," he said.

Lowe got up. "It must be quite sight outside now. . . . I think I'll go and look."

"I'm with you," Macey said. He followed behind with the gun.

Climbing to the lantern room was like leaving a cosy shelter. Even inside the glass frame, the noise was fearsome. When, before Lowe could stop him, Macey opened the door, the wind hurled him back and roared through the lantern like a tornado. It took all Lowe's strength to force the door shut again between gusts.

"Cor . . .!" Macey said. He gazed out disbelievingly through the salt-stained panes. Even from that height, the seas looked immense. They were rolling in from the south-west in great mountains and deep scooped-out hollows, and breaking on the reef in gigantic columns of spray. Salt water showered on the lantern glass like gravel. The whole surface of the sea was in boiling tumult—a great white cauldron seething and creaming round the tower.

Lowe looked at Macey. "How would you like to be down in that lot?"

"Not me!"

"Like Mitchell," Lowe said. "And Robeson . . .!"

"Aw, shut up . . ."

Lowe turned away. "It'll be dark soon. . . . Might as well switch on the light."

A banshee wail drowned his words. Macey cupped his ear. "What you say?"

"The light," Lowe shouted. He crossed to the switchgear. Above their heads, the blazing optic began to revolve. "Now—generator . . ." He pointed downwards, and descended. Macey followed slowly. . . .

Back in the living-room, conditions were now only a little quieter than in the lantern, for the storm was getting up fast. The granite walls were thick enough to keep some of the wind roar out, but the bammering of the waves was louder and the shock of their blows sent vibrations through the whole structure. . . . Lowe talked, while he still could.

"In the old days," he said, raising his voice, "the optics in these towers used to revolve in mercury baths. Sometimes the towers shook so much that the mercury spilled over. Rocked like ships . . ."

There was a crash against the living-room shutter. Macey jumped.

"Spray," Lowe said. "Just heavy spray." He sat down beside the glowing fire. "It's going to be a long, long night. . . ."

Somewhere below them, green water hit the tower with a thud like the fall of a bomb. For the first time, Macey looked uneasy. "Like bein' kicked in the guts, ain't it?"

"This is nothing," Lowe said.

There was another heavier thud. Macey said. "Sounds to me like the place is comin' down. . . . Hope it's built strong."

Lowe shrugged. "It's been up for a fair while, but you can never be sure with lighthouses. There's always the storm that's worse than anyone ever expected. . . . There was a tower along this coast that had been up for years—everyone thought it was safe. The builder—his name was Winstanley—he thought it was safe. He always said his one wish was to be in it in a great storm. And one night, he was."

For a moment, the screeching wind made speech impossible. Then, as the gust passed, Macey said, "What 'appened?"

"No one knows. He was never seen again. Neither was the tower."

"Christ ...!"

"It simply disappeared—swept away like a straw ... But then this is a particularly bad bit of coast. The thing is, there's nothing except ocean between us and America. Three thousand miles of it. ... In a south-westerly storm it funnels into the Channel—tremendous force—like convulsions of Nature—nothing—stand up to it ..."

Lowe broke off. It was hopeless to try and talk any more. The scream of the wind was incessant. He sat listening to it, trying to estimate its strength. It was blowing very hard—force 9, perhaps. More at times. And still rising. . . . Presently he got up and went to the bedroom. From a locker under the bed where Hines was lying dead, he took a roll of cotton-wool. He ripped some of it off, and carefully plugged his ears. It didn't often happen that he felt the need of earplugs, but this was going to be one of the times. He stuffed some more of the cotton-wool into his pocket, and went back to the living-room. He didn't offer any to Macey.

For the last time, he raised his voice in a shout above the tumult. "You—want—any—supper?"

Macey, slumped in his chair on the other side of the fire, shook his head.

The storm continued to mount in violence. There was no rain—just an appalling wind, that rose and rose. By midnight, the noise was no longer a scream—it had swelled to a sustained, deafening roar, like a continuous thunder clap. The wind was hitting the tower now like a solid thing, striking with collision force. There were moments of such elemental fury that the huge seas pounding at the structure seemed to register only as shock and not as sound. Macey's cup and saucer, moved by the vibrations to the edge of the table, fell and broke soundlessly on the slate floor. From top to bottom, the whole lighthouse was shaking and nodding as though in an earthquake.

Lowe had never experienced or imagined anything like it. This really sounded like the ultimate storm. . . . But he had no qualms about the safety of the tower. He knew how cunningly its huge granite blocks were dovetailed into each other and into the living rock. He had absolute confidence in its design—its streamlined, slender upper part; its massive base, spreading out like the bole of a great oak; its high set-off, built to break the worst force of the waves.... Nor did the elements themselves hold terror for him. Respect and wonder and awe—yes. He'd learned that from his coxswain father, and lightkeeping had confirmed the lesson.... Awe amounting almost to worship.... But not terror, which was a cringing thing. As between the muzzle of a gun, and this cataclysmic fury, there was no problem of choice....

All the same, Lowe was beginning to weary. The noise, in spite of his earplugs, seemed at times to pass the threshold of pain. He was beginning to feel a muffling deafness due not to cotton-wool but to prolonged exposure to the battering wind roar. His aching head felt as though it would burst. His body, constantly braced for the shocks, felt sore and stiff. His mind was numbed.... His only consolation, as he looked across the tiny room, was that Macey was in far worse shape....

Macey, the landsman, had listened at first with disbelief to the fantastic crescendo. It couldn't possibly go on like this—let alone get worse.... But that had been right at the start. It had got worse beyond imagining, beyond endurance.... As the hours passed, with no second's respite from the hammering artillery of wind and sea, his face grew white, his head dizzy and sick. He was suffering physically, in a way he'd never known before, a way he'd never thought possible.... He was frightened beyond all reason, because this was something outside all his experience. He gripped the table as shock followed shock, his stomach muscles tight with fear. He couldn't believe that any tower could stand through such a night. He longed for a pillow to bury his head in, but felt so paralysed by the uproar that he couldn't bring himself to move. His nerves were a screaming agony. Sometimes, as the tower shuddered and rocked, his whole body seemed to jerk, as though an electric current had been passed through it.... Once, looking at Lowe through bleared eyes, he opened his mouth, and shouted something, his face a mask of terror—but the storm devoured whatever sound came out. . . . He bent over the table, shaking, abject. . . .

Lowe, watching the disintegration, still waited. He might never have another chance—he must make quite sure. Macey's hand still clutched the gun. . . . Then, as three successive shocks hit the tower, Lowe got slowly to his feet. From his pocket he took the piece of cottonwool he'd brought trom the bedroom. Macey looked up. Lowe pointed to his own plugged ears and held out the cotton wool, making encouraging signs. Macey snatched at it and began to tear pieces off. Lowe turned away. He could see Macey in the wall mirror, stuffing his ears. Both hands occupied. A man in torment, bent only on getting quick relief. The gun on the table. . . .

Lowe swung round and grabbed it.

He leaned back against the thundering wall, pointing the gun at Macey, cocking it with his thumb as he'd seen Macey cock it. . . . Macey made no move at all. He looked as though he didn't even care. . . . His jaw hung loose, his mouth was quivering, his eyes seemed out of focus. He had become, for the moment, a gibbering wreck. . . .

It was three in the morning before the storm showed any sign of abating and nearly six before audible speech became possible again in the tower. Through all those hours Lowe sat motionless against the wall, keeping Macey covered. . . . Watching his slow return to self-control as the bombardment died, watching intelligence and cunning come creeping back into his eyes. . . .

It was extraordinary, Lowe thought, but Macey didn't seem afraid any longer. He'd been reduced to grovelling terror by the elements but he could look almost contemptuously at the barrel of the gun, even though he was at the wrong end of it. . . . The familiar gun. . . .

At last Macey spoke. "You goin' to shoot me, kid?"

"Only if I have to," Lowe said.

"Someone goin' to make you, then?"

"You, if you move."

"Don't reckon you got the guts."

"I wouldn't count on that."

"Don't like guns, do you?"

"No," Lowe said. "But I don't like you, either."

Macey grunted. "What you goin' to do, then . . .? Hand me over to the cops?"

"Of course. . . . As soon as I can."

There was a little silence. Macey seemed to be lost in his own thoughts. Judging by his expression, they weren't altogether unsatisfactory.

"Won't half be a trial, any rate," he said. "One o' them sensational ones, it'll be. All the papers'll be runnin' the story, with great big headlines an' pictures. All the big shots'll be there. I'll 'ave me own counsel, one o' them Q.C. geezers, an' he'll have to do what I say, an' one day I'll be up there in the box meself, tellin' 'em all about it. . . . What's more, they'll 'ave to listen. . . . I'll tell 'em how I shot the manager an' how I shot Mitchell an' how I killed Robeson. . . . Cool, I'll be. . . . An' I'll tell 'em how I took over this ruddy lighthouse an' run it for days, all on me own. . . . First time it's ever 'appened, I reckon. Made 'istory, that's what I done. I tell you, kid, no one won't ever forget 'King' Macey. You hand me over, an' I'll go out in a blaze o' glory . . ."

Lowe shook his head. "Not if I can help it, Macey. . . . When I've told them about last night, you'll be just a murderer who went to pieces when the wind blew. . . ."

Lowe sat a little longer, debating what to do next. He had the gun now—but Macey, with his life forfeit anyway, might not respect it as he had done. Macey was still dangerous—and would be as long as he was free. . . . Lowe thought of Robeson. Perhaps the old man could help him to tie Macey up. . . . But it wouldn't be easy for Robeson, with those bandaged hands. And once Robeson and Macey were close together, it would be risky to shoot. Macey would know that. . . .

No. . . . There was another way. A better way. . . .

Lowe got to his feet. He felt anxious, but his hand was steady on the gun. "Right," he said, "we're going down now. Put your coat on, Macey. . . . Your *own* coat . . ."

Macey took his camel-hair coat from a peg and draped it over his shoulders.

Lowe pointed to the stairs. "After you . . ."

"Where we goin'?"

"You'll see."

Slowly, Macey descended. Lowe followed him, two steps behind, his finger resting lightly on the trigger of the gun, the barrel pointed straight at Macey's back. This was a routine that, in reverse, he'd come to know well. They went down past the store room, down to the entrance door.

"Open it," Lowe said.

"You ain't goin' to put me out there?"

"Open it."

Macey didn't move.

"You can choose," Lowe said. "If you don't open it, I swear to God I'll shoot you now."

Macey hesitated. Then he gave a faint shrug. There was no point in dying before he had to. He opened the door. The wind was strong, but its worst fury was over. Spray still lashed the set-off, but the sea was no longer breaking over it.

"Down the ladder," Lowe said.

Macey started to go down. For a moment, Lowe stood watching him. Then, with a deep sigh of relief, he went back into the tower and secured the door. It was all over. . . .

Robeson was leaning back on his pile of sacks. "Hallo, Jim—I thought I heard you go by. . . . What a night . . .!" Suddenly he was staring. "You've got the gun!"

Lowe looked down at the automatic. "Yes," he said. He hadn't realised he was still carrying it. He closed the safety-catch and laid it on the floor, gently, as though it were a bomb. "I've put Macey on the set-off. He won't give us any more trouble."

Robeson clutched his arm. "Jim, boy, that's wonderful. . . . How did you manage to get it?"

"It wasn't me," Lowe said. "It was what you said, Rob. . . . The wrath of God."

He stayed for a while, giving Robeson an account of the night. He felt little elation—the tower had seen too much tragedy for that. And he was desperately tired. Presently he turned to the door. "I'll bring you some food, Robbie. . . . I'll ring the shore after breakfast."

He went down to the engine room and switched off the generator. In the living-room, he put some more coal on the fire and filled the kettle. Then he went up to the lantern room and turned off the light and went out on to the gallery.

It was a beautiful morning. The sun was just coming up in a pale, clear sky. The sea was subsiding—though its tossing waves were still tipped with white. It would be hours yet before the relief boat could venture near. . . .

Lowe looked down over the rail to the set-off. He couldn't see Macey. For a moment, with an absurd pang, he thought he must have thrown himself into the sea. Then he walked round to the other side of the gallery and saw him. "King" Macey was sitting huddled on the lee side of the set-off, his head buried in his hands. . . . It wasn't, Lowe thought, much of a throne.

www.ingramcontent.com/pod-product-compliance
Ingram Content Group UK Ltd.
Pitfield, Milton Keynes, MK11 3LW, UK
UKHW040105010325
455690UK00002B/17